# THE WITCH HUNTER

# THE
# WITCH HUNTER

## SASHA L. MILLER

# Part I
# Surstuhl

# Chapter One

Mud clung to Ivo's boots as he slogged his way toward what was his best bet for lodging and information. The persistent drizzle that had dogged him all day hadn't let up, and the dreary gray sky didn't seem as though it was going to be clearing anytime soon. Not that a little rain or mud would keep him from his task, but it would be nice to have a sunny day along the way.

It was the wrong season for that, however, so Ivo pushed the stray thought from his mind as he headed for the sprawling, brightly-lit building near the center of the dreary little town that was barely large enough to be marked on Ivo's map.

There was a sign hanging over the door, an affectation the building didn't need. It had a crudely carved boar's head centered on three wooden planks. The sign hung crookedly in the front, swaying drunkenly in the wind, and the rest of the building matched. Despite the light that blazed from the windows, the sills sagged, as did the deck that stretched across the front of the building. For summer gatherings, no doubt, but boots had long worn the whitewash from the planks, and the front of the building could use a new coat or two as well.

Ivo scraped the mud from his boots on the

edge of the steps as he climbed, knocking the worst of it off before he reached the door. Opening it, he stepped into a large greatroom.

Fire burned brightly at the hearth across the room, and lanterns burned throughout the room. A lot of lanterns—but fewer than accounted for the light. Simple magic, which would normally mean nothing, but the small towns of Amersselt distrusted magic and more often met it with violence than reason.

Ivo trudged over to the bar, letting his bag fall to the floor at his feet and slouching onto an open barstool. The room was mostly empty, with a handful of men and women scattered at the tables about the room. There was a serving woman giving orders in the doorway to the kitchen at the back of the room, and a bartender was pouring a beer for the only other man at the bar.

Most of the eyes in the room were on him. He was a stranger, which was something a town like Surstuhl wouldn't see often. They were too far from the main roads and had little of value. Their main resource was lumber and logging, with some fur trades—nothing worth a trek in the rains of early winter.

"Hail, stranger," the barkeep greeted, a hint of unease in his voice as he slid the beer to his patron. "What can I get you?"

"One of those'll do," Ivo said. The barkeep nodded, fetching another wooden cup and pouring beer into it. He brought it over to where Ivo sat, setting it on the bar in front of him.

"You need lodging?" the barkeep asked. "It's a

copper for the beer, two silver for a week's stay."

"Two silver?" Ivo repeated, his eyebrows raising. "You housin' the queen?"

The barkeep laughed at that, giving him an appraising look. "One silver, then. Includes two meals a day, and Annelie will get your things washed if you want."

"And a bath," Ivo said, digging out his coins. "I swear the mud sank through to my bones."

"Mud'll do that," the barkeep said, the coins disappearing beneath his apron almost as quick as Ivo set them on the counter. "I'm Heinrike. What's your name, stranger?"

"Ivo." He took a swig of the beer, not surprised it was decent. Some of the best beer he'd had came from small operations like this. "Good beer."

"Thanks. Annelie makes it. I'll pass that on to her. What brings you to town?" Heinrike asked. "We don't get a lot of visitors out this way, especially this time of year."

"That's the idea," Ivo said. He didn't expound on that. Let the town think he was dodging trouble. It was a better explanation than witch hunting, which always ended poorly whenever he tried to be honest about it. Surstuhl may have witch-powered lights in its inn, but that was no indication that they were any better about magic than any of the other small towns in Amersselt.

"Hmph," Heinrike grunted out, giving Ivo a closer look. "Just don't bring any trouble with you. This is a good town, good people. We don't need trouble."

"I don't aim to bring it," Ivo said. He never did. It always just happened to follow when he rooted a witch out. With luck, the only trouble would be for the witch.

"Good," Heinrike said. "That changes and you'll be sleeping with the pigs, and they snore."

Ivo snorted a laugh and took another swallow of beer. Heinrike was distracted by another patron, and Ivo took the reprieve to glance at the other man sitting at the bar. He was older, grizzled, wearing a thick wool coat with several neat patches sewn on it. His hair was mostly gone, and his beard was trimmed close to his jaw. He toyed with his cup of beer, looking pensive.

Too old to be out working. From the look of the others in the greatroom, they were much the same, or had popped in for a bite before continuing their day. There were several conversations going on, but none of them were interesting. Talk of a roof needing patching, a missing sheep, how long until someone had their baby, and of maybe building a house for a newly married couple, since their respective families were both populous enough it was getting too crowded.

Nothing useful. He'd have better luck later, no doubt, when the town's work stopped for the evening and there were more people to eavesdrop on.

He didn't expect anyone to outright say they were up to black magic, but it would make his job easier. Still, in his experience, most witches were solitary people either living on the outskirts of town or were holed up outside of town, well away from the townspeople they were tormenting.

Draining his cup, Ivo stood as Heinrike made his way back behind the counter. He picked up his bag and said, "I'll take that room now, if it's no trouble."

"No trouble at all. Wench!" Heinrike shouted the last toward the kitchen doorway. The woman in the doorway turned, her eyes rolling as she did.

"What, ass?"

"Got a guest for you," Heinrike said. "Show him a room, will ya?"

Annelie huffed, her mouth pressing together as she regarded Ivo. "You pay?"

"He did. What do you take me for, woman?" Heinrike grumbled. "He wants laundry and a bath."

"Laundry's in two days, but we could do a bath tonight," Annelie said. She crossed the room, the heels of her boots clicking loudly on the wooden floor. "After dinner."

"Whenever's best for you, ma'am," Ivo said. That got him a snort, and she led him across the room to a staircase tucked in the corner. The stairs creaked loudly as they ascended to what proved to be a long hallway. There were a dozen doors along the hall, with hand-carved numbers denoting each one. The walls were painted a light blue that was in much better repair than the whitewashing outside.

Annelie brought him to the fourth room along the hall. "Two meals, served downstairs. The bath will also be downstairs, in the kitchen. We don't drag water up. There's no fireplace in your room or anything fancy—"

"I just want warm water and a place to lay my head, ma'am, nothing more," Ivo said. He tried a smile, but Annelie didn't seem impressed.

"There's a lantern on the table, but more oil will cost you," Annelie warned. "There's fresh linens on the bed. Put anything you want laundered outside your door in two days and we'll get it done."

"Thank you," Ivo said. Annelie took that as a dismissal, casting a last suspicious glance over her shoulder before taking the stairs down to the greatroom. Ivo stepped into his tiny room and surveyed his base of operations.

It was small, barely wide enough to contain the bed, table, and chair that sat within it. The bed was unmade, but true to Annelie's word, there was a neatly folded pile of linen on the foot of the bed. The mattress looked lumpy and uninviting, but Ivo had slept outside in the mud and rain for most of his journey, so he wasn't going to complain.

The room had no windows; it was central to the building, then, and probably one of the warmer rooms. Shutting the door behind him, Ivo snapped his fingers, drawing up a flame in the lantern that rested on the table. Firelight bathed the room, casting long shadows over the sparse furniture. Dropping his bag on the floor, Ivo shucked his thick jacket and draped it over the lone chair. The floorboards creaked as he crossed over to the bed, loud squeals of protest.

Humming under his breath, Ivo quickly and neatly made the bed. Once everything was in place, he dropped down on the bed, keeping his muddy boots on the floor to keep from mucking up the clean blankets.

Tomorrow, he'd be back out in the wet, miserable weather. Hopefully he'd overhear something at dinner that would point him in the direction of the witch practicing black magic. If not, he'd be spending a lot of time wandering the woods in the mud and rain. Ivo grimaced at that thought. At least it wasn't snowing yet, though it wouldn't be long coming. He wanted to root that witch out and deal with them before the snow came, but Ivo rarely got what he wanted.

If he did, he'd be tucked up at the library in the capital city, Roesschot, digging into old texts on magic and weathering visits from his mother. And spoiling his nieces and nephews. Hopefully he'd be back by the time the winter festivals started; he'd hate to miss them.

All he needed to do was catch and deal with this witch, and then he could return to Roesschot. With luck, Captain Alderling would consider that enough for the year. This witch wasn't a big fry, but they were casting spells that Alderling had found alarming, and so Ivo had been sent.

Sighing, Ivo bunched the pillow up under his head. He could head out now, but that might raise suspicions. If he was going to keep up the ruse that he was running to Surstuhl to keep away from trouble, the last thing he needed to do was go right out to find it like he was here for a reason.

No, he'd nap, and then spend the evening drinking and eavesdropping. It was a much better idea than going right back out into the mud and rain.

*~*~*

That evening, Ivo stationed himself in the

middle of the bar. He deflected questions about what he was doing there, focusing on learning more about the town and the people who lived there. He spoke with Decker, a logger with a ruddy face and a penchant for drinking beer a cup at a go. He seemed more than happy to chat, covering everything from the logging efforts to the poor apple harvest to the best houses to hit up if Ivo wanted something other than Annelie's soups and stews.

"Not that there's anything wrong with Annie's cooking, mind," Decker said, setting down his empty cup. Heinrike was almost immediately there with another cup, swapping the full for the empty without a word before hurrying off to serve another patron. "But Gabriele's got a mean hand for kneading up—"

Before Decker could finish that thought, the door burst open and a young man burst in. His hair was askew and his face and vest were covered in a layer of soot. "Fire! In the east grove!"

The greatroom exploded with noise, and Ivo followed the cue of most of the people in the room, standing and heading for the door. His jacket was upstairs, but working to put a fire out would certainly keep him warm. The thought that it was perhaps witch fire gnawed at Ivo's mind, but for what reason would a witch set a fire so publicly?

"Again?" someone ahead of Ivo was asking. "That can't be coincidence."

Ivo meandered closer, ignoring the shouted commands from someone near the front of the line to listen closer to the man's conversation.

All the man's companion did was shake her head though, giving him a quelling look. "Don't speak of it. You'll bring more trouble down on yourself. Evert did, and look what happened to him. If you start, what would Ingo do?"

The man scowled, but apparently took the admonishment to heart, stepping up to start filling a bucket.

Again, he'd said, so someone had set a fire previously. In the same place? And something had happened to Evert, something... permanent, Ivo was willing to bet, given the way the woman had said it. Ivo tucked that information away to investigate further later and joined the line of bucketeers. The fire appeared to be natural, not magic-inspired, so either the witch was smart enough to use magic to set the fire but not sustain it, or it was regular arson. Ivo would have to sort out which in the morning, as there would be no way to inspect the grove—apple trees, he thought he heard someone mention—without arousing suspicion.

At least he'd been tucked away in his room at the tavern the whole day, so no suspicion should fall on him. He'd had that happen before, if the townfolk found out he could work magic, and sometimes simply because it was easiest to blame the new face. Those had not been his most successful missions. At least there had only been the once that he'd been chased out of a village with pitchforks and people screaming for his head... That had probably been his least successful mission.

He'd gotten better at being discreet since then, thankfully. The last time he'd given away his magic, all he'd gotten were a few death threats, though it probably would've been worse if he'd not taken out the witch terrorizing the town first.

The walk back to the tavern after the fire was out was quiet, with a few murmured conversations about delaying work in the morning, but nothing about what might have caused the fire or anything more about it being an additional fire. How often were the fires occurring? What was the goal? Things to find out later. For now, he'd give anything for a fresh beer and a few minutes to let his arms stop feeling like they'd been wrung through a washer.

The tavern was mostly empty when Ivo stepped into it. It appeared most of the folk who had been enjoying an evening beer had decided to head home after the excitement of the fire. Ivo couldn't blame them. He was ready to fall into bed, and would eagerly after a last attempt at getting some info.

Ivo returned to his bar stool, slouching tiredly on the counter. Annelie appeared from the back; Heinrike was likely still making his way in. Wordlessly, she poured him a beer, giving him an appraising eye. "Thank you for the help."

Ivo shrugged. "Always better to put a fire out than leave it to spread."

"Not your town, Mister..." Annelie trailed off.

"Ivo. You can call me Ivo. I don't care for my surname." Ivo drank half the beer in one swallow, and before she could speak again, asked, "Someone mentioned that's not the first fire you've had."

"It's not," Annelie said. "You don't have to worry about the place burning down around you, if that's your thought. They've all been out in the apple groves."

"It would make for an unpleasant night," Ivo

said lightly. The way she said it, *they've all*, made it sound like more than two. So there had been many fires, and all in the apple groves. That meant the apple groves would be the place to start in the morning. He drank down the rest of the beer. "Thanks for the drink."

"Rest well," Annelie said. She stared after him as he went to climb the stairs to his room, but Ivo didn't pay it any mind. He climbed upstairs slowly, weariness settling in as he ascended.

He'd never minded witch hunting. It was honest work and did immeasurable good for the towns and communities he helped. He only wished, for the thousandth time, that he had help doing it. His sister had helped him for several years before she'd met her husband and settled into Roesschot to have children and build up their shop making and trading herbs, poultices and charms.

He didn't fault her for it, but he did miss her presence. Alderling had tried assigning him partners now and again throughout the few years since then, but none of them stuck. They were either magic-deaf or too young and cocksure to be of any use. Ivo had given up on the idea of a partner after his last one had nearly gotten them both killed by trying to tackle a witch who was casting an incendiary spell. Ivo had gotten several new scars from that stunt, and Katrin had barely survived her idiocy.

The last he'd heard, she'd settled into a desk job doing research, so maybe she had learned her lesson. It wasn't a lesson Ivo cared to let anyone repeat, though, so he'd told Alderling he'd only continue if he did so on his own. It was safer.

It didn't stop the road from being lonely, but it did help ease the guilt he had over the injuries and curses his previous partners had suffered. Ivo let himself into his room, shutting the door before he lit the lantern. Sitting down on the edge of the bed, he leaned down to remove his boots. There was mud caked on them, but he wasn't going to offend Annelie any further by knocking it loose inside the room.

"Apple grove," Ivo muttered, lighting the lantern and leaned over to pull out his notebook from his bag. It leaned against the wall by the bed, untouched since he'd dropped it there earlier. Tapping the flimsy lock on the front, Ivo charmed it open and flipped through the pages until he came to a new page. He jotted down a few notes: the date he'd arrived, a few thoughts on where to start.

Shutting the book, he tapped the lock again to secure it. He didn't carry the key, and only magic could break it, so he was sure it would stay undisturbed. If it didn't, well, that would certainly reveal a magic user in the town.

As far as Ivo knew, there wasn't any magical significance to apples, though there might be an emotional connection for the witch. That could be as good a fuel as actual magic components. In the morning, when he went out to the apple groves, he'd be able to sort out whether the fires had any magic purpose. It was always possible that the fires were simply a coincidence, that the town had someone who liked to play with fire, but Ivo thought that unlikely.

Tossing the notebook on the table, he yawned and lay back on the bed. It wasn't bad, for a tavern that likely saw little in the way of guests. Stretching out, Ivo pulled the blanket up over him and settled in to get some rest.

# Chapter Two

The apple groves were east and north of town, large and sprawling and certainly a feature that Ivo would've expected to have heard of before he'd reached the town. All Alderling had said was logging, so perhaps the apples were a secret the town kept to itself.

Crunching through dead leaves, Ivo was grateful the mud wasn't as thick here. The trees on the eastern end were blackened by the fire, and Ivo took a moment to survey the them. They were tall, had obviously been growing for decades. There were leaves sparsely clinging to the tree branches, but no sign of fruit. Picking season would've been a few months previous, Ivo thought, but he wasn't positive. He'd never had much interest in farming or harvesting. He could see charred trunks further into the grove as well, and Ivo hummed thoughtfully.

Ivo tugged off one of his gloves, the cold biting at his fingers as he reached toward the closest charred trunk. Some of the bark crumbled under his touch. He reached out with his magic softly, carefully feeling out the edges of the soot-crusted tree. Nothing. It had been a normal fire.

Which only meant that magic hadn't been used to create it. If it was the work of the witch, there was every possibility that the fire fed another goal. Dusting the soot off his fingers, Ivo wandered further into the grove, lazily heading toward the next charred spot. It was twenty feet from the charred bit of trees Ivo had inspected first. It was an older fire; the ground had long since absorbed the soot. It had burned hotter or longer, to judge by the way the trees no longer had any bark on them, and a few had died.

There wasn't anything different about the burned trees deeper into the grove, but Ivo spotted another blackened set of trees. He wandered closer, letting his magic loose to feel out any residue from the witch's spells. It could be some kid in town setting fires for fun, but after the townsman's comment the previous night about not getting involved, Ivo doubted it.

The only problem was that there was no residue. The fires burned normally, and they fed no larger spell that Ivo could find. So why was the witch burning the grove? They weren't even burning the whole of the grove, just small clusters of trees here and there.

Maybe it was a distraction. Ivo and the townsfolk had been thoroughly focused on putting out the fire the previous night. Perhaps there was something happening elsewhere at the same time that the witch was attending to. In any case, Ivo was finding nothing of use in the grove. Reining his magic back in, Ivo stared thoughtfully at the burned trees in front of him. He could traipse about the forest for days, but that wasn't likely to get him very far very fast.

Time to go ask more questions. Maybe he

could find someone in town who was more willing to talk than Annelie or Heinrike. Both of them had had little to say on the fires when Ivo had brought it up again at breakfast.

Turning, Ivo stopped, frowning at the footsteps in the mud. There were more tracks than just his. He'd been paying so much attention to the trees he hadn't noticed that before. The new footprints crossed Ivo's tracks, heading toward the edge of the grove and into the forest proper. Ivo started after them, curious as to who would be wandering around the grove and forest when there were no apples to be harvested.

It could simply be someone from town out to forage in a quieter part of the forest. The tracks were fresh, none of the evening's drizzle having misshapen or erased them. It could be the witch's footprints as they left the grove after getting whatever it was they needed from the previous night's fire. Ivo slid his hands into his jacket pockets, palming the small switchblade he kept inside.

He kept alert as he approached the forest's edge, but there was no additional sign of the person he was tracking, only the footprints in the mud. Ivo didn't pause as he reached the forest, following the tracks in until the ground firmed up and the mud disappeared. There were a few sloughings of mud ahead of him, but after that, any trace of the person disappeared.

Ivo debated for a moment, and then decided it would be worth it to keep going. He could always question the townsfolk later, after all, and maybe the trail would pick up further into the forest. Ivo pushed through the undergrowth, uncaring if he left his own trail as he walked. Maybe he was tracking a hunter; that would explain why there was little in the way of a trail to follow. Ivo spotted the occasional boot imprint and broken twig, but nothing a casual walker would leave in the wood.

Only a hunter, or a witch trying to avoid being followed.

Ivo listened carefully for any sounds that might indicate his quarry was near. There was a low hum of insects, the occasional birdsong, the burbling of a distant brook, but no sounds that indicated Ivo was doing anything other than wasting his time.

The brook grew louder as he walked, and he wasn't surprised when it finally appeared, a small, fast-moving stream of water rushing through a break in the trees. The mud was back along the bank, and so were the footprints—they appeared on one side, and then hopped the brook to the other side. Ivo grimaced, stifling the superstition that tried to deter him from crossing the water. It was *not* bad luck to cross moving water, and he knew it.

It didn't stop the hair on the back of his neck from rising as he jumped the brook. He glanced around, but it was just his mind playing tricks on him. There was no one around, and he didn't need to burn any hettlewood to get rid of the bad luck.

The footprints trailed off after a few feet as the ground firmed up again. Rubbing at the back of his neck to make the strange feeling go away, Ivo set off in that direction, annoyed at himself for dithering over the brook. He'd barely made it a few steps into the trees before a voice spoke from above.

"Well, well, a stranger in the forest. How unusual."

Ivo snapped his head up, frowning at the man who sprawled in a tall tree with several thick limbs in front of Ivo. He was dressed in brown and dark green, to better blend in with the forest, no doubt. His hair fell around his face, a sun-kissed brown, and sharp brown eyes studied Ivo intently.

The witch? Perhaps, but Ivo doubted it. He'd never had a witch approach him; he'd always sought them out. Still, better to be cautious than underestimate his opponent. If Ivo knew anything, it was that witches were nothing if not unpredictable.

"Is it?" Ivo asked. "Where do you usually find strangers?"

"In town, where else?" The man grinned, and in the shadows of the tree, Ivo couldn't tell if the expression was welcoming or threatening.

"Not up trees?" Ivo asked. Had the man climbed the tree to surprise him? Why else would he climb a tree?

"Well, I didn't find you in a tree." The man tilted his head at Ivo, and Ivo had the distinct feeling he was being teased. "Do you make a habit of climbing trees, mister..."

"Ivo. My name is Ivo." When the man didn't immediately reply, he prompted, "And yours? Unless you prefer to be called tree man."

"That does have a nice ring to it," the man said, apparently considering using that moniker seriously. Finally, he said, "My name is Hansel." He said it with enough weight that it was clear he expected Ivo to know who he was and to associate something negative with that name.

"Hansel," Ivo repeated. "I don't know why you're saying that as though it's a terrible name. It's perfectly respectable. My sister named her son after a bird. You could do worse."

Hansel snorted, sitting up and eyeing Ivo curiously. "You're not from these parts, are you, Ivo?"

"We've established that," Ivo said. He slid his hands into his pockets, casually loosening the sheath of his knife. "Remember? You called me a stranger when I walked up."

"Mmm, yes," Hansel said, swinging his legs over the side of the thick tree branch he was sitting on. "But you must be from farther afield if you haven't heard of me."

"What should I have heard about you?" Ivo asked, sliding the knife from its sheath. Not that a knife would do much against a witch, if Hansel was one and decided to use his magic to attack. Ivo had a few tricks up his sleeves, but hopefully he wouldn't need to use them.

Hansel laughed, sliding from the tree and landing on his feet in front of Ivo. Tensing, Ivo braced for an attack... but Hansel just dusted off his trousers. "Stick around, Ivo, and I'm sure the fair townspeople of Surstuhl will fill you in. They're pretty chatty when it's gossip that doesn't involve them."

"Really," Ivo said. Maybe he could get Hansel to talk, though if he was the witch, that might be an error. Ivo wasn't getting that sense from Hansel, but it wouldn't be the first time he was wrong. "I didn't get that impression. They seemed to mostly talk about how hard they work."

Hansel laughed again, flashing his crooked, not-quite-amused smile again. Derisive. That was it. Hansel obviously didn't have a high opinion of the town. "I'm sure they worked very hard yesterday."

"Because of the fire?" Ivo asked, falling into step when Hansel began walking toward the brook. Hansel's steps were quiet, and he seemed to effortlessly avoid anything that would give away his steps: fallen leaves and twigs, squelching in the mud, stepping too hard against the firmer ground.

"Another fire?" Hansel asked, his mocking tone suddenly gone. He frowned pensively. "Where?"

"The grove," Ivo said, becoming surer that Hansel was not his witch. He seemed genuinely unknowing of the fire. "It didn't get far, and only a handful of trees were affected, so far as I know. It was pretty dark."

Hansel didn't reply to that, hopping over the brook without hesitation. Ivo followed, gritting his teeth as he crossed the water. They continued back through the forest toward the grove. Ivo wondered where Hansel had been the previous night; it had seemed like the entire village had been out to deal with the fire. He didn't remember seeing Hansel, but he also didn't remember most of the people he'd seen that evening.

They reached the edge of the grove before Hansel spoke again, pausing in his quick, quiet steps to shoot Ivo a suspicious look. "You forget what you were doing out there in the wood?"

"No," Ivo said. He almost said he'd been tracking Hansel, but that was undoubtedly the wrong thing to say. "I'm just wandering around. You seemed interesting enough to follow."

Hansel snorted. "Wandering is dangerous around here. Don't go too deep into the wood."

"Oh?" Ivo asked, following again when Hansel began to walk into the grove. "Why not?"

"It's dangerous," Hansel repeated. He glanced around, as though looking for someone who might be eavesdropping. "Surstuhl is being afflicted with bad luck."

"I had heard that much, but I've run into my own streak of bad luck. Maybe the two will cancel each other out," Ivo suggested, keeping up with the lie that he was here because he had fallen on hard times. Add a hint that he was potentially hiding from something or someone, and that was plenty enough for the townsfolk to gossip about without thinking him a witch—or a plant from the Crown, which had happened once. That town had had more than witch problems.

"I doubt it," Hansel replied darkly. "Being here is likely to make that bad luck worse. I'd move on quickly if I were you."

"Would you? So why haven't you?"

"I live here," Hansel said, flashing Ivo a smile that was very unfriendly. "You don't."

"Would you like me to show you where the fire was?" Ivo asked, changing the subject. Hansel's smile slipped into a scowl, and he stared at Ivo with no less suspicion than he'd displayed so far. Without waiting for an answer, Ivo started toward the edge of the grove. "This way."

Hansel followed, though it was only because the ground was so muddy that Ivo could hear his steps at all. For all other intents, Hansel was silent. Ivo didn't prompt him, giving him time to stew as they approached the newly-burned section of trees.

"Here," Ivo said. The trees still smelled charred, the unpleasant smell of burned wet wood wafting up from the trunks and branches that had been scorched. Ivo surveyed them again, but like before, there wasn't anything unusual for him to note. "Have any kids in town who like to play with fire?"

"It's not a kid," Hansel said flatly, gingerly touching a half-burned trunk. "Kids would've been caught by now."

"So who do you think it is? Or what?" Ivo asked. Hansel shrugged, moving between the trees and frowning up at the boughs above them.

"It's bad luck to talk about it, don't you know?" Hansel asked. He grabbed a low-hanging branch and swung up into the tree, climbing up swiftly and surely, as though he'd done it before. "You climb trees, Ivo?"

"I can," Ivo said, though he doubted he'd be as graceful as Hansel was about it.

"Come see why it's dangerous to talk about, then." Hansel gestured for him to climb. Ivo hesitated—he really wasn't keen on tree climbing, but so far Hansel had been more forthcoming than the rest of the village. Still, he didn't trust Hansel. There was something about the man Ivo couldn't put his finger on.

Hansel grinned, that wicked, taunting smile that gave his face a mean cast to it that didn't suit him at all. "Are you chicken?"

"I haven't climbed a tree since I was a wee

lad," Ivo grumbled, and the grin on Hansel's face morphed into something more genuinely amused.

Hansel snickered, patting the trunk. "It might be scorched, but it's plenty steady. Even for a man of your bulk."

"Bulk, hah," Ivo muttered, approaching the tree. He was bigger than Hansel, to be sure, but he wasn't so large that he'd break the limbs. Hansel was lean and lithe, while Ivo was stockier, a 'work horse' as his sister liked to tease.

Ivo frowned at the tree, loosening a few buttons on his thigh-length jacket so that he could more easily move. Well aware that Hansel was watching his every move, Ivo grabbed the low-hanging branch that Hansel had used to swing up into the tree and started his climb.

It was more accurate to call it a scramble, as his boots didn't catch on the tree trunk, sliding down the ash-coated bark as he tried to get purchase. Hansel watched, looking more and more amused as Ivo clambered up after him. It took Ivo almost three times as long as Hansel had taken to get up to the same level, and when Ivo did, he leaned heavily on the tree, his breathing more strained than he'd like to admit.

"What am I looking at?" Ivo asked, staring out into the grove. He could see several patches of burned trunks, as he'd noted earlier, but nothing stood out. Were the burned patches done in some sort of pattern? That could be the true purpose of the witch's fires. If they were burning the trees in a pattern to cast a larger spell...

"This," Hansel said, tapping the trunk, close to

where he balanced on a thick tree branch. There, at the juncture where the branch met the trunk, was a palm-sized sigil, carved into the trunk and glowing a faint gold.

"A witch symbol," Ivo breathed. It was obviously still live, given the glow, but why hadn't he been able to suss it out? He looked at Hansel, aiming to gauge his reaction—and found himself being watched by Hansel in turn. Hansel was waiting for his reaction. "You have witches around here?"

"Only one," Hansel said. Then he paused, adding with a grin. "I think."

"You think," Ivo repeated, skeptical. "Why do you have a witch? What did Surstuhl do?"

"I'm sure there's plenty of reasons for a witch to set up residence around here," Hansel said, shrugging. He gave the sigil a last look, then started climbing down the tree.

"Like what?" Ivo asked. He wanted to inspect the sigil more, but it would be better to do that later, after he and Hansel had parted ways. He started to climb down, much more slowly and gingerly than Hansel.

"We don't get many strangers here," Hansel said. He landed on the ground, brushing off his trousers again, and grinned as Ivo nearly slipped off a branch when it sloughed a burnt bit of bark under his boot. "Test your steps before you put your weight on your foot."

"Thanks," Ivo said dryly. He made it back to the ground after another moment, and thankfully no more slips. "That's all it takes to attract a witch?"

"Well," Hansel drawled, leaning in toward Ivo

conspiratorially. "I've heard some rumors."

"Rumors about what?" Ivo asked. As happy as he was to be getting this information, he was suspicious—why was Hansel being so forthcoming?

"A curse," Hansel said, laughing when Ivo gave him a skeptical look. He smacked Ivo on the shoulder, and then headed deeper into the grove again. "Ask around, Ivo. I'm sure the townsfolk will be more than happy to tell you all about it."

Ivo almost followed after him to ask more questions, but Hansel's body language didn't invite his company. Perhaps he could get some more information from the townspeople, now that he had a starting point. Did anyone else know about the sigils? Unlikely, though they'd definitely decided there was something afoot.

As soon as Hansel disappeared between the trees, Ivo sighed and casually leaned against the tree they'd climbed. He reached out with his magic, feeling for the sigil... and there it was, buried beneath the tree's life force. It was weak, barely there, and whatever it had been meant to do, it had already done. The only things remaining were the mark and a small amount of energy. The energy didn't go anywhere, so there was no trail to follow.

What it was supposed to do was beyond Ivo. Sighing, he glanced around. There was no one in sight, so he started climbing the tree again. He was a little faster on the way up this time, and he leaned in to study the sigil as soon as he had it in his sights. It was a simple thing, several horizontal lines intersected with diagonal lines. Ivo committed it to memory, and then dug out his knife and carved a large X through it. There wasn't enough energy in the sigil for it to fire back at him, thankfully, and it winked out, the light dying before he was finished carving through it.

Ivo climbed back down carefully, glancing around again, but the grove was still deserted. He could go back to town... but it was probably better to check the other trees, to see if any of them carried the witch's mark. Ivo reluctantly started trudging toward the nearest burnt cluster of trees, sighing at the thought that he was going to have to climb more of them to find out what was going on.

# Chapter Three

Ivo groaned as he sank into the bath, the hot, lye soap-scented water easing his mind. It was almost too hot, but Ivo wasn't going to complain about that. He was alone in a small room off the kitchen, where there was some weird furnace set below the tub. The water still needed to be hauled in by hand, but Ivo hadn't minded helping, since it meant he could have a hot bath after his day traipsing around in the forest.

Annelie had seemed grateful for that, though she hadn't had much to say, as usual, and she'd favored the mud Ivo had tracked in with a look that could've blistered the paint off a royal carriage.

Ivo's mind drifted back to the sigils in the forest. They had all been identical, all glowing faintly and all in the center of the burned trees. Ivo wasn't sure if he'd done the smart thing in destroying them, but his other option had been to leave them and let them continue whatever harm they might have been doing.

Scrubbing a hand through his beard, Ivo ran through the basic sigils. They'd looked familiar, but they weren't the typical energy leech spells Ivo was used to dealing with. They'd had something to do with the fires, but the 'what' of it was eluding him.

He needed more information. Annelie and

Heinrike were out; they'd both continued to dodge his careful questions. If he pressed harder he'd be sleeping in the woods, and that never agreed with him. Maybe he could convince someone else to talk. He could buy someone a few drinks, provided there wasn't another fire or other emergency to draw the crowd out of the tavern.

His thoughts strayed to Hansel, and he wondered again what Hansel had been doing in the woods. Why had he shown Ivo the sigil? Did he suspect Ivo was the witch plaguing the town? It was possible, but Hansel seemed to know more about the cause than he wanted to let on. He'd mentioned a curse, but had he meant the town's general bad luck or a more specific curse spell?

He'd ask Heinrike about Hansel. Heinrike had been slightly more forthcoming than his wife; maybe he'd share something about the strange woodsman that would give Ivo more insight.

Picking up a washcloth, Ivo started to clean the mud and dirt from his skin, relishing the hot water and soap as he scrubbed himself red. He soaked in the tub for a while after he was clean and took the time to trim his beard. He'd had his hair trimmed up before he'd left on this adventure, so he wouldn't need to worry about that for a while.

Once he ran out of reasons to linger, he climbed out of the tub and dried off, then dressed slowly in the cleanest clothes he had left. He was looking forward to clean laundry as well. There were plenty of things Ivo enjoyed about traveling, but the lack of baths and clean clothes were not among them.

Ivo returned to his room briefly to stash his

dirty things and the bar of soap he'd brought to the baths with him, and then headed back to the greatroom. Heinrike had a cup of beer ready for him by the time he sat down in his usual spot. The room was half full, plenty of the laborers having returned from their work to drink and enjoy a warm meal. Likely those without a spouse to go home to, or those where all the adults spent their days out working.

"So what did you spend your day doing?" Heinrike asked, leaning on the bar. He seemed to be asking out of idle curiosity, but there was a spark of suspicion and wariness in his gaze that belied the casual tone to his voice.

"Wandering," Ivo replied. It wasn't a good answer, and would do nothing to allay any suspicions that Heinrike had. "I ran into an odd man. Said his name was Hansel?"

"Oh, he decided to show his face again?" Heinrike said, snorting. He leaned away from the bar, glancing around to see if anyone needed a fresh beer.

"I suppose. He doesn't live in town?" Ivo asked, surprised to hear that. He'd assumed... Maybe Hansel was his witch, after all. But if so, why show Ivo the sigils?

"He does. When he wants. He and his sister..." Heinrike coughed, his mouth twisting. "He lives at the edge of town, in his family's old house, but he more often is cavorting about in the woods."

"He has a sister?" Ivo asked. Maybe he could find out more about Hansel from her.

Heinrike shrugged, like he was somehow uncertain of that. "He's bad news. I'd stay away from him, if I were you."

"Noted," Ivo said. He didn't agree. "Have I met his sister? Should I stay away from her too?"

"No, you haven't," Heinrike said, obviously reluctant to continue the conversation. He glanced around again. "She's miss— She's run off. You won't meet her." Annelie appeared in the doorway to the kitchen, and Heinrike said, "Excuse me," before hurrying away to talk to her.

Ivo let him go, sipping at his beer. He could guess why the townsfolk were reluctant to talk about the bad things that were taking place in town. Bringing it up could bring trouble down on their heads. Still, if Hansel's sister was missing—because surely that was what Heinrike had wanted to say— wouldn't that warrant getting help somewhere? Were any other people missing? Was Hansel wandering around in the woods looking for her? Was *she* the witch?

Downing the rest of his beer, Ivo stood and made his way to a nearby table. "Mind if I join you?"

The two women at the table, both obviously in from a hard, dirty day of work, looked at him and grinned in tandem.

Ivo spent the evening hours chatting with the them, learning very little other than that they both worked on a logging team and were unmarried. They were dismissive of the 'rumors' of witchcraft when Ivo brought it up, laughing it off. The younger one seemed to think the fires were the work of a kid, maybe that von Adleberg brat, he was always looking for attention.

The older woman seemed to think it was a lightning strike, followed by opportunism by the town's mayor, who had apparently only narrowly kept that title after the apple harvest had failed.

"Third year in a row," Adal said, her mouth twisting in a grimace. "Annelie used to make an amazing mead out of those apples, but there's been only little, sick apples the last few years. I hope it turns around soon. Maybe a burning is just what the grove needs to cull the weak trees."

"I doubt it," Liezel said, drinking back some of her beer. "I think we need to start a new grove entirely, not just burn a few trees here and there. None of them are budding. I know there's plenty of folk in the cities who would love the wood we'd get from those trees."

"We can't turn them into lumber," Adal argued. "They're part of the town's history."

"We could use them in town," Liezel suggested. "They'd stay here, we'd get to spruce things up, and we could plant new trees that aren't sickly. Keep the heritage, fix the problem."

"I guess, but you'll never get anyone who could make that decision to agree to it," Adal said. She huffed. "The people in charge like that where you come from, Ivo?"

"Worse," Ivo said cheerfully. "There's more of them, and they endlessly debate everything. Even planting one new tree would take months of hemming and hawing."

"Ugh," Liezel said, wrinkling her nose. "That why you left? Don't want to deal with the talking?"

"I don't mind talking," Ivo said. "No, I left because... well... I had a deal set up with some people and it didn't work out. They weren't very happy about it, so I decided I'd find somewhere else to be for a while. Somewhere quieter."

"I don't know about quiet," Adal said. She shrugged her shoulders, then stretched her arms up over her head. "Surstuhl might've been quiet once upon a time, but it isn't much for that these days. I don't know I believe these witch rumors, but someone is up to something. Just keep your head down. Come on, Liezel, we should get going."

"Early mornings," Liezel explained to Ivo, standing when Adal did. "You're welcome to join us if you want some work."

"I might do that," Ivo said. It could be a good way to further integrate himself into the town. It would be much less suspicious if he was working and seeming like he was trying to stay, instead of simply poking around town with no discernible reason. "Though I'm not sure I could do the hard work you do. I'm awfully soft." Ivo patted his belly, which had a nice layer of fat on it.

That got him a laugh from both of them, and Ivo waved as they left, sipping at the rest of his beer as he thought about their words. There was a witch, no matter what Adal and Liezel thought. Likely their homes and families hadn't been affected much, if at all, by the magic the witch was working.

He hadn't gotten a chance to ask about Hansel or his sister, but if he joined Adal and Liezel in the morning, he could ask then.

Or he could sleep in and do some more digging around town, and then do some work. He could already feel several aching muscles from his trips up and down the apple trees. An extra day of rest before he tried to be a logger couldn't hurt. He might be able to come up with some more things to quiz them about in the interim.

Climbing slowly to his feet, Ivo stretched and then headed back to the bar. The greatroom was mostly empty, the patrons heading home after their meals and beer. Ivo set his empty cup on the bar, waving Heinrike away when he moved to refill it.

"I'm heading to bed," Ivo said. He dropped a few coins on the bar. "Thanks for keeping me in beer."

That got a smile out of Heinrike, who wished him a goodnight as he scooped the coins off the bar. Ivo headed up the stairs, making his way back to his little room. It was warm and cozy, the fireplace below running up through the wall behind his bed heating it well. Ivo took the time to gather his laundry for Annelie and then collapsed into bed.

His thoughts ran around in his head for an age before he finally drifted off to sleep, thoughts of the sigils and Hansel's missing sister following into his dreams.

*~*~*


Ivo walked slowly up the aisle of the small temple, his footsteps echoing quietly in the empty building. There were several benches set up throughout the room, arrayed in almost straight lines. The temple was tucked in the back of the town, near the forest's edge, and it was sheer luck that Ivo had stumbled across it. The building was in good repair and obviously cleaned regularly, despite the lack of anyone in the building. The door had been unlocked, and Ivo would lay good coin that there was no priest or priestess in town.

Surstuhl was too small for that. Maybe it had been bigger once, big enough to warrant a member of the clergy. Maybe they had had a member of the town leave to train at one of the major temples and return to establish and maintain the temple.

It smelled of spices and fresh air, with bundles of plants hanging from the rafters and light shining through the dozen windows that were set into every wall. The altar was laid out as was appropriate, with offerings to each of the three gods: dried flowers for Aurora, the goddess of the harvest and new life; burnt applewood for Phillipe, the god of the afterlife and rebirth; and dried fruit for Mirjam, the goddess of health and peace of mind.

Ivo inclined his head at the altar. Someone in town cared enough to maintain the temple, that was clear, and there was even a small table with several books behind the altar. Ivo walked over to that, curious. There were the usual fare, books of children's tales, a few copies of the prayers of the gods, and one journal detailing the harvests and logging efforts over the last nearly thirty years.

Picking up the journal, Ivo settled on the nearest bench and flipped through it. The first few years had been normal, apparently, with plenty of apples and other crops. The goats and sheep had done well, with only one death in the birthing season. Five years after the start of the journal, however, something changed. The harvest grew scarce, more sheep had died, and there were fewer births. That continued for two years before the crops and livestock suddenly rebounded. Ivo kept reading, but there was no mention as to why those two years had been bad.

The records continued, mostly normal, until Ivo reached the last year. As Adal and Liezel had said, the harvest had failed. There were the same hallmarks as the previous famine: fewer births, fewer crops, more animal deaths. Had there been a witch twenty-something years back too? Or was that simply a coincidence?

"You show up in strange places."

Ivo nearly jumped out of his skin, barely maintaining his composure. He swiveled on the bench, throwing one leg over it to fully face Hansel. "Why is it strange to visit a temple?"

"You didn't strike me as the sort who practiced," Hansel said. He was dressed much the same as he'd been the previous day, in browns and greens that would blend easily into the forest.

Ivo didn't reply to that, studying Hansel instead. He looked tired, his hair askew as though he'd slept on it in a strange position, and dark circles under his eyes.

"What? Not going to tell me that I know nothing about you?" Hansel asked, walking further into the temple. He approached the altar, running his fingers over the smooth wood.

"You don't, but you know that," Ivo said, shrugging. He shut the journal, wondering if he should ask Hansel about the previous famine. Had Hansel even been born then? He looked young, twenty, twenty-five at the most. He might have been born, but he probably would've been too young to remember it. "How old are you?"

Hansel frowned at him, obviously taken aback by that question. "Why are you asking?"

"There was a famine..." Ivo consulted the book, "... some twenty-three years ago. Were you old enough to know about that?"

Hansel's expression darkened. He repeated, his tone harsher, "Why are you asking?"

"Curiosity," Ivo said, keeping his tone level. Hansel obviously knew something, though would he share?

"I was old enough," Hansel said. "Why did you destroy the witchmarks in the trees?"

Ivo raised his eyebrows. He hadn't expected Hansel to climb back up into the trees. "Never a good thing to leave a witchmark to fester."

"No other reason?" Hansel pressed. He crossed his arms, his sharp brown eyes unerring as he stared at Ivo. "Not looking to take out the witch and take her place, are you?"

"You know who the witch is?" Ivo asked, latching onto that. Hansel had said her, which was more than Ivo had known.

"Are you a witch?" Hansel asked. He grinned, a feral expression. The thought that Hansel looked better when amused flashed through Ivo's head. "See, I can avoid answering questions too."

Shaking away the stray thought, Ivo considered his options. He could try and get Hansel to answer his questions without giving him anything in return, but the stubborn set of Hansel's jaw suggested that was a poor option. Hansel was more likely to decide he was a witch and needed to be gotten rid of alongside the other witch. Not that Ivo thought he could; Ivo was no pushover, and it didn't seem as though the townsfolk held a great deal of respect for Hansel.

Best to come clean. Well, mostly clean. Hansel didn't need to know that Ivo was a witch.

"I'm here to stop the witch," Ivo said. "She's been casting spells that caught the attention of the wrong people—for her. I've been sent to find her and stop her."

"Hah," Hansel said, but some of the tension leaked from his shoulders. "What spells?"

"I don't know," Ivo said. He didn't. Alderling hadn't had that information. "I usually don't. It doesn't matter, in any case. All that matters is that a witch is practicing black magic in this area, and that's illegal and needs to stop."

"What proof do you have? How can I be sure you're not making this up?" Hansel narrowed his eyes, then asked, "You usually don't know? How often do you go witch hunting?"

"Lots," Ivo said. He shrugged, standing up to return the journal to the table. "I have no proof. It's better to travel without documents, and I shouldn't be telling you this at all. If the witch catches wind of what I'm up to, it could undermine my ability to find her." He paused, frowning at Hansel. "You know who it is?"

"No," Hansel said. He grimaced. "Maybe. I don't know."

Ivo set the journal down where he'd gotten it and turned back to Hansel, waiting for Hansel to elaborate. When Hansel didn't, Ivo said, "I know that your sister disappeared. There was a famine two decades back that seems to bear all the hallmarks of this year's poor harvest. The witch is doing something to the apple groves, though I haven't seen those sigils—witchmarks—before, so I don't know what."

Hansel sighed, running a hand through his unruly hair and looking all the more tired. He trudged over to the nearest bench and sat down heavily. He braced his elbows on his knees, looking pensive.

"Do you know anything about the previous famine? Was it a witch problem or just poor years?" Ivo asked. He stayed by the table, not wanting to intrude on Hansel's space.

"It was a witch," Hansel said. He rubbed his hands over his face. "Exactly like this. Well, not exactly. I was five, my sister was seven."

Which made Hansel near thirty. "What happened?"

"We killed her." Hansel said it simply, glancing up at Ivo with dark eyes. "We thought."

"You, as in the town, or you, as in you and your sister?" Ivo asked. He didn't see how two small children would have been able to kill a witch, but Hansel nodded.

"My sister and I." He took a deep breath. "My stepmother was desperate. The famine had affected the whole town, and there was no money, no food. So she tried to leave us in the woods. We made it home the first time, but the second..."

"The witch found you," Ivo said. What kind of parent would leave their children in the woods? Even if Hansel's stepmother hadn't cared much for children not her own, leaving any child alone in the woods to forage was the worst kind of crime.

"She did," Hansel confirmed. "She wanted to eat us, but she had to do... something first."

Maximize the power she got from it, likely. There were preparations and incantations and other such steps that could be taken to maximize the power from eating a child or a young woman. They had the most potential for power: children for their youth, women for their ability to bear children. Supposedly.

"She made Gretel clean house and locked me up, threatening that she'd kill the other every day if we didn't do as we were told. One day she started having Gretel make a large fire, in the center of a circle of witchmarks. She unlocked my chains and started bringing me over, but I guess she didn't expect Gretel or I to fight back." Hansel paused, glancing at Ivo before looking away again. "We pushed her into the fire. She was old and slow. She screamed, but Gretel and I didn't stop to see if she... died. We ran, and somehow we managed to find ourselves home again. My father had kicked out my stepmother for leaving us in the woods, and after that, everything went back to normal."

"Until this year," Ivo said.

"Until this year," Hansel repeated. "The harvest failed again, Gretel went missing..." He trailed off, staring down at his feet. "I've tried to find her, to find the witch, but I've had no luck. She could be dead."

Ivo didn't know what to say to that. "Maybe, but she could be alive. Do you think it's the same witch?"

"Who else could it be?" Hansel asked bleakly. He shook his head. "I should go."

"No," Ivo said, stepping forward. "Let me help. I'm going to be looking for the witch anyway. I can help look for your sister too."

Hansel looked as though he was going to deny Ivo's help, staring at him with a suspicious, wary look. He'd probably asked for help from the town and been rebuffed. What did the town think had happened to Gretel? Did they really believe she'd run off like Heinrike had tried to say?

"Fine. Let's go, then." Hansel stood and headed from the temple, his steps as quick and quiet as they'd been in the forest. Shaking his head, Ivo followed after him, hoping he didn't regret revealing to Hansel why he'd come to Surstuhl.

# Chapter Four

Hansel's home was small and cozy, set on the edge of town and well-tended. Mostly well-tended, Ivo revised as he followed Hansel toward the door. The plants in the window boxes were growing unkempt, in need of a trim. Some were herbs, and Ivo recognized a few plants that were mainly medicinal in nature. Hansel opened the door and stepped inside, and Ivo followed, pausing on the threshold of the home.

It smelled dusty inside but was neat and tidy. The house was all one room, centered around a giant hearth to Ivo's left. A ladder led up to a loft, where the sleeping quarters no doubt were. The house might need a good airing, but it didn't appear as though anything was wrong otherwise.

"How did she go missing?" Ivo asked, stepping into the house and shutting the door behind him.

Hansel shrugged. "There's not much to tell." He crossed the room to the large counter set against the back wall. "Tea?"

"Sure," Ivo said. He glanced around the house. The furniture was plain, if sturdy-looking, and there were several knitted throw rugs laid out across the floor to help ward against the winter chill.

"About two months ago, Gretel went out hunting. She never came back." Hansel fussed with a kettle, moving over to the hearth to get a fire going. Ivo could've had it roaring in seconds, but despite the impulse, he knew better. Hansel was the last person Ivo would want to know that he was a witch.

"What does the town think happened to her?" Ivo asked, choosing a kitchen chair to sit down on.

"That she ran off to a big city, never mind that she took nothing with her," Hansel said, sneering. He slowly built up the fire, not looking at Ivo. "Some think she was killed by the wildlife. She's only been hunting since she was thirteen, so obviously more than a decade of experience hunting means nothing."

"Any other theories?" Ivo asked.

"Some think she was taken by a witch," Hansel said. He finally looked at Ivo, anger plain in his expression. "But they won't do anything. They'd rather keep their heads down and hope the problem goes away. It did last time, after all. Just a few lean years, and then everything will go back to normal. If it takes Gretel dying, well, what's one person?"

"I see," Ivo said softly. It wasn't the smartest course, and it wouldn't save them, but he could understand it, to a certain degree. Magic in towns like this was unknown, scary. In the minds of most, it was better to not court trouble. "No one else has gone missing? I heard something about Evert?"

"No, no one else has gone missing. Evert is just an idiot who likes to blame the world for his problems," Hansel said. He stood, adding a few last branches to the fire. He grimaced. "No one's gone missing yet. I'm sure it's only a matter of time. I can only hope she's still alive and that's what's keeping the witch from going after anyone else."

"Very possible," Ivo said. "Have you found anything in the woods? Other than the witchmarks in the trees?"

"No," Hansel said. He scowled, pacing the room. "I've covered all of Gretel's usual hunting grounds. I've looked and looked for the cabin where we were captured as children, but I can't find it."

"It may have moved, if the witch is strong enough," Ivo said, seeking to be reassuring. Hansel's efforts weren't in vain. If the witch was hiding from him, she was spending more energy than she was likely able to recoup doing so. In which case, she'd need to refuel more often. But if she wasn't kidnapping children or young women—more than Gretel, and that was supposing that Gretel wasn't the witch herself—then how was she getting her magic restored?

From the trees. Ivo nearly kicked himself. That should've occurred to him sooner. The trees in the apple groves had been under attack for ages. What if the witchmarks weren't to cause the fires but were causing the fires? If the witch was drawing energy from the trees and miscalculated, there was every possibility they would combust, overloaded by badly structured magic. That would leave the witchmark, residual energy to make the witchmark glow, and also break the connection between the witch and the spell.

The only way to test that theory would be to return to the grove and check other trees. Ivo might be able to get a read on where the witch was if he could find a witchmark connected to her... but he couldn't do that with Hansel in tow. He didn't want to explain how he'd gotten a read, not when Hansel was so obviously opposed to magic.

"What else have you done?" Ivo asked. Hansel moved to collect the kettle before joining Ivo at the small kitchen table. They spent the next hour drinking minty tea and discussing what ground Hansel had covered and where they might go next.

"What do you remember about the witch from when you were younger?" Ivo asked, finishing his cup of tea. He wasn't going to rule out the possibility that the witch from Hansel's childhood was the same witch they were dealing with today, though it seemed unlikely. More likely was that Gretel had run off to practice black magic in the woods. Why, Ivo didn't know, but it was more likely than a witch from over twenty years ago suddenly re-emerging to torment Surstuhl again.

Hansel twisted his cup between his hands, frowning down at the minty tea. He'd been subdued since he'd walked Ivo through what he'd done to track Gretel. He hadn't even found her bow, apparently. "She was tall. I know I was a child, but she seemed taller than most people I knew then. Thin, like she never ate. I never remember seeing her eat, either, but that doesn't mean she didn't."

"She could have been subsisting off her magic. It would explain why she wanted to eat you and Gretel."

Hansel grimaced at that. "Ugh. Who eats children?"

"Black magic witches," Ivo said. "Do you

remember anything else?"

"She always smelled of burnt meat and sweets," Hansel said. He shrugged, his mouth twisting unhappily. "I don't know what you're looking for. I would say you should ask Gretel, but she's not here."

"We'll find her," Ivo said, standing up. "Come, daylight's wasting. Have you searched the trees in the grove? Or have you only looked at the burned ones?"

"Only the burned ones," Hansel said. "Why? Do you think there's witchmarks on the rest?"

"It's possible. Worth looking at, in any case. Unless you have a better idea." Ivo didn't relish the idea of traipsing through the woods without a direction in mind, and there wasn't any harm in checking out the trees in the grove with Hansel. He wouldn't trace the magic, but he could certainly see if his theory was correct.

"Let's go," Hansel said. He didn't bother to clear up after their tea, heading for the front door. It was his house, so Ivo followed suit, even as he chafed at the idea of leaving dishes out to attract insects. Hansel obviously didn't care and was nearly at the door before Ivo could fetch his jacket from where he'd hung it on the back of the chair.

Outside, the air was biting, nipping into Ivo's skin as they walked toward the apple grove. Ivo pulled on his gloves, watching curiously as Hansel did the same. He didn't seem to notice the cold much, even though the jacket he wore was much thinner and lighter than Ivo's. He spent much of his time outdoors, though, so likely he didn't feel the cold as sharply.

Hansel was quiet as they walked, lost in thought, and Ivo let him be. He wanted to probe, to ask Hansel more questions, but none of them were relevant to the witch or finding Gretel. Thankfully, as fast as Hansel walked, they reached the grove quickly. Hansel delved into the trees without pausing, going straight to a cluster of untouched trees. They bore no leaves nor fruit, but they also hadn't been affected by the fires.

Ivo waited on the ground as Hansel scaled the tree, in no hurry to repeat the awkward climb of the previous day. Hansel climbed the tree like he did it every day, pausing on each branch he scaled to inspect the bark. It took several minutes, but eventually he climbed down, shaking his head.

"Nothing there."

"So much for that," Ivo said. He frowned, at a loss. What were the witchmarks for, then?

"They're not in every tree. I only found them in a few of the burned ones," Hansel said. He headed toward a nearby tree. Ivo really should've thought of that; of course not every tree would have a sigil. Not only would that have been time consuming, but it wouldn't be necessary to pull energy from the grove, provided there was enough sigils to create a web. Ivo walked closer to the tree Hansel was inspecting. He could help, but he really did hate climbing trees.

Ivo settled for inspecting the branches he could see from the ground. He doubted the witch was stupid enough to leave a sigil where the whole town could see it, but he'd seen stupider things before. He was just looking at his third tree when Hansel jumped out of the tree he was in, seemingly barely making it to the neighboring tree.

"Are you insane?" Ivo demanded. It was bad enough to climb the trees, but jumping between them? That seemed an invitation to falling and breaking something.

Hansel only laughed, crouching down in the tree. "Probably. Here's one."

Ivo strode over to the tree in question, eyeing the limbs in the tree. There didn't seem to be any low-lying branches, and Ivo scowled. "How am I supposed to get up there? And don't suggest that I follow your route. I don't care to break my neck today."

Hansel grinned, leaning down. "Grab that branch and I'll help you up."

Ivo still hesitated but finally conceded. He needed to see the sigil if he was going to be of any use. Grabbing the branch Hansel indicated, Ivo took Hansel's hand and scrambled up, bracing his feet on the tree trunk and using Hansel as leverage to pull himself up. He nearly toppled them both out of the tree, but at the last moment Hansel gave a yank that pulled him up far enough he could put his feet on something solid.

"I really dislike trees," Ivo grumbled. He was acutely aware of Hansel's proximity, the pine-and-cinnamon scent that seemed to cling to his jacket, and his smile was nothing but trouble that Ivo didn't need.

"I've noticed," Hansel said, his grin hiding all traces of the troubles he was facing. "The witchmark is here."

Ivo redirected his attention, relieved to have

the distraction. There, in the bark at the junction of the trunk and one of the larger branches was the witchmark.

It looked like the others, glowing faintly and carved past the layers of bark on the tree and into the wood. Ivo ran his fingers over it, frowning, and then let loose his magic. Just a little, enough to get a read on the spell.

Like he'd suspected, it was a life draining spell. He'd have to use more power to figure out where the energy was going, but he wasn't going to do that with Hansel sitting inches away from him.

"It's just like the others," Ivo said. "It must be an energy draining spell, though it's not one I've seen before. Adapted to pull energy from the trees, maybe."

"How do we break it?" Hansel asked intently. A knife appeared in his hand with a twitch of his wrist, startling Ivo.

"Where..." he started to ask, but that wasn't important. "No, don't break it. It's still active, and it could backfire on us."

Hansel shifted irritably. "So we just leave it there?"

"For now," Ivo said. He hummed thoughtfully, trying to figure out the best way to proceed without raising Hansel's suspicions. "I want to check on something. I brought a book with me that might have some information on how best to break the spell. It might be linked to the other trees in the grove, which would make it more dangerous to break. It could physically throw you from the tree."

Hansel grimaced, flicking his wrist and

making the knife disappear. "I guess. Maybe we should burn the whole grove down."

"That's the other problem. If we break the witch's hold on the grove, she'll be forced to find something else to use for energy," Ivo said. He paused, wondering if he should clarify. It wasn't the worst plan... The witch would be forced out of hiding, but Ivo would prefer to try and track her down without anyone else getting caught in the crossfire.

"You mean people," Hansel said, his voice holding a wealth of disgust. "Right. So what do you suggest, then, oh great witch hunter?"

Ivo snorted. "Getting out of this tree, for one."

"Hah," Hansel said, but he seemed to agree. He helped Ivo back down out of the tree before following, landing on the ground with a soft thump. Ivo frowned at the trees.

"Any other trees affected? Or just the apple grove?" Ivo asked. It would make more sense if more trees, maybe even livestock, were affected, but no one had mentioned anything like that so far.

"I don't know," Hansel said. He scowled. "I hadn't been looking for that. Just Gretel."

"So what blooms or gives fruit this time of year? Or over the last few months?" Ivo asked. "We could check those out. That could give us the scope of how much energy this witch is drawing."

"What does she need this energy for, anyway?" Hansel asked. He scrubbed a hand through his hair, looking frustrated. "That's what I don't understand. What spells is she casting?"

"Youth, health," Ivo said immediately. Those

were the hallmarks of black magic. "Black magic is anything that steals energy or life from other people, animals, or plants."

"All magic is black magic," Hansel muttered. "Is that it? That seems incredibly short sighted. What happens when she runs out of victims here? The trees aren't going to last long at the rate she's burning them."

"I doubt the burning is intentional." Ivo hesitated, then decided a quick defense wasn't completely out of order. "Not all magic is black magic. If it draws from the caster only, that's simply regular magic. It's more limited, which is why so many witches turn to black magic. It also can't restore youth and health to the witch casting it."

"If you say so," Hansel muttered. "What good will looking for more trees do? Does it matter how big the witch's reach is if we can't find her?"

"If we know how big it is, it'll be easier to figure out how to target the spells and draw her out," Ivo said. It wasn't the best plan, but with Hansel right there, and his obvious negative attitude to any and all magic, Ivo didn't have a better plan. "Do you have a map of the town and the surrounding area?"

"No," Hansel said. He shrugged. "We don't really need maps around here. Everyone knows the area."

"I don't," Ivo said with a grin. "Come on, let's go get something to eat and you can draw me one. Show me where you've been and where else we can look."

Hansel didn't look entirely thrilled by that idea, but he obligingly followed Ivo out of the grove and back into town. His face turned into more and more of a thundercloud as they approached the tavern, but he entered the greatroom behind Ivo without hesitation. Ivo chose a table near the fireplace, where a fire burned steadily. He took off his jacket and slung it over the back of a chair, sitting down in it afterward. Hansel kept his jacket on, though he did unbutton it and tucked his gloves in his pockets.

He seemed like he was about to take off, and he kept glancing around the room as though he was cornered. Ivo nodded to Heinrike when he glanced over, and Heinrike set about pouring them two cups of beer. When he brought them over, he barely looked at Hansel, who was... glaring at him like Heinrike was personally responsible for Gretel's disappearance.

"Could we get something warm to eat?" Ivo asked pleasantly.

"Sure thing," Heinrike said, hurrying away like his shoes were on fire.

"What's that about?" Ivo asked as soon as Heinrike disappeared into the kitchen.

"He started the rumor that Gretel ran off to one of the bigger cities," Hansel said. He looked like he wanted to set the entire tavern on fire, and Ivo made a note to ask Heinrike about that later. Why would he start a rumor like that?

"We'll make this quick. I'm sorry, I didn't realize there was bad blood between you and Heinrike," Ivo said. He pulled a notebook out of one of the jacket pockets, flipping to a blank page. "I figured it would be easier to do this inside, where it's warm and ry."

"I guess," Hansel muttered. Heinrike arrived with two bowls of a steaming soup and a small plate of biscuits, which he set on the table and then almost immediately disappeared. No doubt Hansel had had words with him about the rumor, and Heinrike was avoiding a repeat.

Hansel ignored the food to start drawing a map. He drew for a moment on one page, then scowled at it and flipped the page to start again. Ivo bit his lip against a caution; he only had so much paper. Hansel seemed to work better the second time, drawing several circles around each other. He tapped the center one.

"This is the town," he said. "Here's the groves." He pointed to a circular oblong he'd drawn above and to the right of the town. "Gretel mostly hunted out here." He tapped the pencil against the paper past the woods.

"Where's your home?" Ivo asked. He'd lost his bearings after leaving the temple; Hansel hadn't led him down any tracks he'd followed before.

"Here." Hansel made an 'x' on the page on the south side of the village circle. "I've searched out her hunting grounds and south of the house, but I haven't found anything."

"Do you remember even a vague direction to the witch's house from when you were younger?" Ivo asked. That was probably a stretch. Even if Hansel did know, there was no saying that it was there anymore, or that the witch didn't have it obscured so no one could find it.

"No," Hansel said. His mouth twisted

unhappily. "The best I could remember was some of the trees around the house. The fruit on them looked like sweets, which is why we went toward the cottage in the first place. Gretel got us home the second time my stepmother left us in the woods."

And she wasn't available to help. Maybe, if Gretel wasn't the witch and Hansel's theory that the old woman from his youth was still around, she'd been kidnapped to keep anyone from finding the cottage.

It seemed unlikely, though. If she'd been old when Hansel and Gretel had been her captives twenty years previously, he doubted she would've survived to terrorize the town now, not without doing the sort of black magic that would've affected the town.

"So what do you suggest we do now?" Hansel asked. He dragged the bowl of soup close, starting to eat slowly. "Searching the woods isn't getting me anywhere."

Ivo hummed thoughtfully, picking up a biscuit and taking a bite. The best option would be to trace the energy spells. That wasn't an option he could do around Hansel, though. "You really believe this is the same witch from your youth?"

"I do," Hansel said, bristling. "Why? What do you think?"

"I think if she was that old when you pushed her into the fire, it's unlikely she survived this long. Unless she had some other means of sustaining herself." Ivo dunked his biscuit in his soup. "So either someone else has set up shop, or the witch moved and came back. Are there any other towns in the area? Anyone else besides Gretel go missing recently?"

Hansel glared at Ivo like he'd told Hansel it was his fault there was a witch. Or that it was his sister. "If you're insinuating that Gretel could be the witch, then I definitely don't need or want your help to find her."

"That's not what I said," Ivo said, straining to keep his patience. "Did anyone else go missing? Before the grove started failing, before the fires."

Hansel took a deep breath, stabbing his spoon into his soup. "Right. Let me think."

Ivo focused on eating, letting Hansel simmer with his thoughts. Hansel was vehemently sure his sister wasn't a witch, and the more Ivo thought about it, the more he agreed. It was hard to hide the work of black magic. The apple grove had been affected for longer than two months, so it was likely not Gretel's work. But if she'd been missing for two months, at the hands of the witch, it was unlikely she was still alive. He'd keep that to himself though. Hansel didn't seem like he'd take that well.

"No one has disappeared in the last year, other than Gretel," Hansel finally said. "I don't think anyone has left, either, though you might want to ask around about that. I didn't pay much attention to people's comings and goings."

"Any nearby towns?" Ivo asked. He finished his bowl of soup and reached for another biscuit.

"One. Aramore. It's an hour's hike to the west."

"All right," Ivo said. That was probably the best bet to find out more without using his magic.

"Then let's go to Aramore."

# Chapter Five

Adamore was smaller than Surstuhl, Hansel explained as they hiked along a poorly-trod trail through the forest. It was apparent that very few people made the trip between the two towns.

"That's because Adamore was founded after a feud between two families about two generations back. There's enough bad feelings still that most people don't make the trip, and we're far enough away that it has to be urgent," Hansel said. "No one's ever told me what the fight was about."

"When was the last time you've seen someone from Adamore?" Ivo asked, stumbling over a rough patch of roots that had grown into the trail. He'd been doing that a lot, much to his annoyance. On his own, he was usually much more graceful. Walking this path, however, following after Hansel, seemed to be making his feet scuff and catch on every third step. Hansel seemed to have no such trouble, walking the path without any hesitation.

"I have no idea," Hansel said. He shrugged, glancing back with an apologetic look. "I prefer to spend my time in the woods. I can't remember the last time someone came from out of town before you. It's been years, I can tell you that."

Maybe a better question for Heinrike. If he'd

talk to Ivo after seeing him talking to Hansel.

"What do you do in the woods? Hunt?" Ivo asked, inclined to keep the conversation going. Because he wanted to keep himself distracted from the witch hunt, or maybe because he wanted to know more about Hansel. It could be useful later, after all.

"Sometimes. Not often. I don't have the patience for it. Mostly I explore," Hansel said. "Gather herbs and mushrooms and anything that might be useful. I tend the temple too, and sometimes help the farmers with the crops or birthings."

"A jack of all trades, then," Ivo said.

"I guess," Hansel said. He didn't sound particularly thrilled by it.

"Don't enjoy it?" Ivo asked. "I've always preferred doing a dozen different things throughout the year rather than be tethered to one task."

"It's all right," Hansel said. He paused in walking, glancing around, and Ivo caught the hint of a frown on his face when he caught up.

"What is it?" Ivo asked. He listened, snaking out a bit of magic to see if something was off. Nothing magical seemed off, but there was very little sound in the forest itself, which did seem odd.

"I'm not sure," Hansel said. He started forward again, and Ivo followed, wincing every time he made noise. Hansel was quieter, and he frowned more and more as they walked. The path was growing worse, more overgrown, but Hansel wasn't deterred, continuing forward more slowly but still confident in his step.

"How close are we?" Ivo asked in a low voice after what seemed like an age of silence.

"Should be about there," Hansel said, his frown furrowing his brow. He didn't say anything more, but Ivo didn't need him to explicitly state that something was off. They walked on, and after a short while, the trees and undergrowth began to thin out, until they emerged into a clearing.

Into Adamore. Ivo stared, taken aback.

The town was in shambles. There were a few dozen houses and cottages before them, and every last one of them looked abandoned. There were a few stray, scrawny chickens roaming the trod-dirt streets, but otherwise there was no sign of life. The wind kicked up, bringing the scent of rot and wet leaves on the air.

"This..." Hansel started to say, but shook his head and started into the small town. Ivo followed after, reaching out to feel for magic. Still nothing, just as there had been nothing in the woods. But if the witch had... already completed whatever she had done here, there wouldn't have been any magic to feel.

They checked all of the houses, but each and every one was empty. There were no people, no animals save the few stray chickens pecking around the dirt road.

"This isn't good," Ivo said, breaking the uneasy quiet. "I don't understand why an entire town would disappear. How, rather. A single witch couldn't take out an entire town like this, not if she was still weak."

"There wasn't much town for her to take out," Hansel said. He scrubbed a hand through his hair, looking distressed as he stared at the empty village.

The path in the center of the houses was covered in undisturbed leaves and browning grass, as though no one had walked it in months. "There was a sickness. It hit both Adamore and Surstuhl, but we weathered it better. They lost half their people."

"When?" Ivo asked. He doubted it was related, but it couldn't hurt to be sure.

"Three years ago. Long before any of this started. There were maybe two dozen people in Adamore after the illness passed," Hansel said. "That was one of the last times I remember seeing anyone from Adamore in Surstuhl. They came for help, after several town members died of the illness."

"Not since," Ivo said. He sighed. It was entirely possible the witch had lured the villagers to their deaths, one or two at a time. She could have trapped the rest of them, and while men or older folk weren't ideal, they would still serve to give her some energy. It was possible the witch even came from Adamore, since Ivo still thought it was unlikely that the witch from Hansel's childhood was still alive if they hadn't heard from her in almost twenty years.

"Not that I know of," Hansel said. "Are they all dead?"

"Probably," Ivo said quietly, trying to soften the blow. "I don't know for sure. Maybe they all decided to leave after the illness swept through."

"Maybe." Hansel didn't seem convinced.

"Let's look around, see if anything can give us an idea of what happened," Ivo said. He glanced at the sky. They'd lose light in another few hours, and they still needed to make the trek back to Surstuhl. "Let's split up."

"Is that safe?" Hansel asked. "What if..." he trailed off, not seeming to have a specific threat.

"This place is long abandoned," Ivo said. "It should be fine. Better than staying here overnight or coming back again tomorrow."

Hansel conceded that with a grimace. He gestured to the far houses. "I'll start there, then. You start here. We can meet in the middle."

"Yell if you find anything," Ivo said. He headed toward the nearest house, opening the door and stepping inside. It didn't seem odd, initially. Like Hansel's home, it was one large room with a loft for sleeping. The whole place smelled of dust and dirt, and the back door was cracked. There was dust on nearly every surface, and leaves and some dirt had blown in through the back door. The room was tidy otherwise. No signs of people leaving in a rush.

Ivo stepped inside, leaving the front door open behind him. He poked around the house, tracking dust everywhere, and all he found was signs that no one had ever left. If they had, they hadn't bothered to pack a single thing. There was money, valuables, clothing and food. All of it was tidy, neat, put away as though the owner planned to return. The food was rotted and moldy, some of it sludge instead of anything resembling actual food.

There was no sign of magic. Not a single sigil and no traces of energy when he reached out, even when he went a little deeper, hidden from Hansel's discriminating gaze.

Leaving the first house, Ivo walked to the second. He spotted Hansel entering another building across the little town, a troubled look on his face, but he didn't pause, so he must not have found anything pressing.

The next house was the same as the first. Everything was covered in dust, nothing was out of place. The only odd similarity was that the back door was open as well. Ivo frowned, heading toward it. He stepped outside, but the back of the house didn't seem any different from the front. The ground was littered with wet, rotting leaves; there was a stack of neatly chopped firewood against the back wall; and the door shut easily, so it wasn't broken.

Moving to enter the house, Ivo stopped when he saw the sigil. It was small, carved in the center of the door at the top edge, and had he been a little shorter, he might not have seen it. It didn't glow, and when Ivo reached out his magic toward it, there was no energy left in it. The spell had already been completed. Leaning closer, Ivo studied the mark. It looked like a sleeping enchantment, which would explain why there were no signs of a struggle inside the house.

Leaving that house behind, Ivo trekked back through the rotting leaves to the first house. He wasn't surprised to find a similar sigil on the back door. So the witch *had* taken out the entire town.

That seemed improbable, but what else could a sleeping charm on every house in town mean? Though two houses having a sigil wasn't exactly the whole town. Best to keep looking, but a sense of dread was sinking into Ivo's bones. He fought the impulse to find Hansel and get out of Adamore. That wasn't going to help anything, even if the idea of lingering in a ghost town made him uneasy.

Shaking off the jitters that were making the hair on the back of his neck raise, Ivo headed to a third house. He went in via the back door, somewhat surprised there was no sigil on the door. Unlike the first two houses, the back door was shut tightly. So maybe this house had been empty already? Ivo stepped inside, his eyes widening. Unlike the previous two houses, this one was a mess. There were clothes and blankets tossed haphazardly across the floor, and various bits of furniture were strewn across the home. It looked as though someone had taken the time to dismantle the furniture but had left bits and pieces of it behind.

Ivo stepped further inside, scoping for sigils, but found none. He frowned, cautiously making his way through the mess. There was no rhyme or reason to the destruction that he could find. Unlike the first two homes, there was no food in the kitchen. The blankets and clothing were dusty and smelled as though they'd been damp or had spent months in storage. There were no personal effects. It didn't add up, and Ivo didn't like that.

He spent a few more minutes looking around the house, before letting himself out the front door. Walking around the house Ivo found no sign of any sigils. This house hadn't had any spells cast on it, or rather, its occupants hadn't.

Perhaps it hadn't had occupants? Maybe it was unoccupied after the illness Hansel had spoken of, and it had been ransacked for supplies, either by the witch or by the other townsfolk. Ivo shook his head and started toward the next house.

He met Hansel in the center of the town, at

what appeared to be a community hall. It was a large, open building with what looked like the remnants of several chairs and tables. The walls were decorated with hand-made wreaths of dried flowers and vines. Hansel looked troubled, but Ivo didn't blame him. The town was empty, with sigils on most doors and many of the houses ransacked for furniture.

"What did you find?" Ivo asked. He walked the hall, checking for sigils as he went. He didn't expect to find any, but there was nothing to be hurt with thoroughness.

"A mess," Hansel said. "Most of these houses are a wreck, but not like the people living here left in a hurry. Everything they would've taken with them, clothes, treasures, food... it's all still here."

"I found the same," Ivo said. "There's a few places that are fine, but most of them are a mess. There's also a sigil—a witchmark—on many of the doors. Not all of them, but anywhere it seemed like people had been living."

"I saw that too. Should we mark them out?" Hansel asked. He had stayed by the door, though his gaze followed Ivo's movements around the room.

"No point," Ivo said. "There's nothing left to them. They were meant to make anyone inside the dwelling sleep, and the spell has been cast and completed."

"Then why did you destroy the witchmarks in the grove?" Hansel asked. "Weren't they dead?"

"No," Ivo said. He gave up his inspection of the hall, having found nothing suspicious other than the broken furniture. "They still glowed. There was still energy there. My theory is that the witch was pulling energy from the grove, but was doing so poorly, and the spells occasionally unbalance and overload, causing the grove to catch fire. I'm not positive, but I don't know what other reason she'd have for marking so many trees. There's nothing to be gained, that I know of, from setting random patches of the apple grove on fire."

Hansel nodded. "We done here?"

"Yes and no," Ivo said. He sighed, glancing around in frustration. "I feel like I'm missing something."

"I know," Hansel said. "Why is everything such a mess? Did she kill everyone? Why is the furniture dismantled?"

"I don't know," Ivo admitted. "This isn't like anything I've seen before. Just the scale alone. You said there were two dozen people living here after the illness, and that's probably accurate. There's enough houses with sigils to support that."

Hansel headed for the door, heading outside. The sky was growing overcast, and it only added to the dreary atmosphere of the abandoned town.

Ivo the town, hoping answers would jump out at him. Not literally—the last thing he wanted was to be attacked by a witch in the middle of a ghost town, even if it would put things to rest quickly. Could he handle a witch who had sacrificed two dozen people? Ivo pushed that thought aside, resisting the urge to reach for his protective charm.

Hansel shrugged. He shifted his weight, still looking uneasy, but Ivo didn't blame him. Standing in the middle of Adamore was unnerving. "Is there anything else you want to look at, or should we head back? I don't relish the idea of taking that trail in the middle of the night."

"I don't think so, unless there's anything you want to show me." The witch was likely based in the woods somewhere nearby, but Ivo doubted they'd have time to search her out while there was still daylight, and the only thing worse than the idea of staying in Adamore for the night was the idea of facing the witch in the middle of the night.

Two dozen people. Ivo followed as Hansel wordlessly headed back toward the forest, his mind whirling with the little information he had. There were no answers to his questions yet, only dread that he was facing something out of his scope. He could write Aderling, but any help would be a long time coming, and how long before the witch struck at Surstuhl?

Well, he'd write Aderling anyway. He could dig deeper, try to find answers, and then figure out whether he could wait for help or not. He didn't say anything to Hansel, but if the witch could make two dozen people disappear, it was increasingly unlikely that his sister was still alive. On the plus side, it was also unlikely that Gretel was the witch. Somehow, he figured that would be cold comfort to Hansel.

The trip back through the forest was filled with tense silence. It seemed to take even longer to return to Surstuhl than it had to get to Adamore, but Ivo didn't complain. He watched his steps, let his thoughts tumble, and tried not to worry too much. Still, it was a relief when he and Hansel split up at the town's edge after agreeing to meet up again in the morning to continue their search.

Ivo headed back to the tavern, letting himself in and heading immediately for the stairs to the second floor. Heinrike waved, looking like he wanted to talk, but Ivo only returned the wave and headed up the stairs. He'd chat with Heinrike later. He wasn't sure whether to discuss Adamore or not. Better to feel it out carefully. He didn't want to incite a panic or bring about undue questions about why he was there.

Maybe it would be better to warn the people of Surstuhl. Give them a chance to leave... but that would decimate the town and anyone who stayed behind. Ivo sighed, entering his room and shutting the door behind him. He stripped off his jacket and fell onto the bed, his thoughts still racing. If he didn't warn people, their deaths would be on his hands if the witch attacked the town.

If he did warn people, it could tip off the witch, ruin the town, or get him thrown out on his ear for stirring up trouble.

He'd ask Hansel. Maybe he could give Ivo some advice or insight on how the town might react. He didn't think asking Heinrike or Annelie would get him anywhere. He could also probe Adal and Liezel. They might not believe it was a witch... which was another problem. If he did warn Surstuhl, how did he go about convincing them that the threat was real?

Adamore. That was strong evidence.

The other problem was that given enough panic, the town might turn on him. It would be easy enough to point to the stranger and pin their troubles on him. It wouldn't matter that he'd only just arrived. What would matter was that he was an easy target.

He'd keep it to himself for now. Until he'd

gathered more information and could better warn the town. He'd also ask Hansel. Sighing, Ivo closed his eyes and let himself rest. He'd figure the rest out later.

# Chapter Six

Ivo sat down at the bar, wincing at the noise around him. He'd woken up after a brief nap with a raging headache, and all he wanted to do was crawl back into bed and hide there. The haunting vision of the ghost town of Adamore lurked behind his eyes every time he closed them, however, and he had entirely too much to do to sleep away the rest of his evening.

"Evening," Ivo greeted Heinrike, who was quick to bring him a beer. Ivo passed over a few coins, enough for that evening, and sipped at his beer.

The greatroom was mostly empty; Ivo must have hit the point in the evening where most of the loggers had headed home, leaving only a few stragglers sipping beer around the room. Heinrike leaned on the counter, looking pensive.

"Annelie and I were chatting earlier, Ivo," Heinrike began, and Ivo already didn't like the way this conversation was heading. "We were wondering what you were thinking of doing here."

"What do you mean?" Ivo asked, taking a deeper swallow of beer.

"Well, we saw you talking with Adal the other night," Heinrike said. "That's a good line of work, if you're able."

"I haven't decided if I want to stay yet," Ivo said, not sure what Heinrike's motives were. Maybe he was just trying to keep Ivo away from Hansel. But to what end?

Heinrike leaned closer. "Well, don't listen to that superstitious woodsman. He's so busy gallivanting about the woods that he wouldn't know a real problem if it hit him in the face."

"Oh?" Ivo said, keeping a straight face. Obviously there was no love lost between Heinrike and Hansel. "I just said I'd help him look for his sister. Sounded better than logging for a day's work."

"Hah." Heinrike snorted. "That no-good sister of his probably ran off to the nearest city. She never was satisfied with Surstuhl, even though it's a good town. Good people."

"You think she would've left without telling her brother? From his descriptions, they were pretty close," Ivo said. He sipped at his beer, filing away everything Heinrike was saying. It wasn't true, of course, but maybe Heinrike could give him some more details on Hansel and Gretel that Hansel might not give away.

"I am surprised she didn't take him with her, but maybe they had a fight. They did that every so often. I'd see one or the other sulking about for a few weeks." Heinrike shrugged. "But him running around sowing rumors of a witch is dangerous. It might cause a panic."

"He said there was a witch a few decades back, when he was a child?" Did the town think there had been a witch? Or had they dismissed it then, too?

"Of course he did," Heinrike said dismissively. "Flights of fancy. Don't get me wrong, it was a damn shame their stepmother tried to lose them in the woods, but they were young, and no one ever found any evidence of some magical cottage in the woods. They never were the same after that. Damn shame."

"Ah," Ivo said. So the town thought Hansel and Gretel had made the witch up. No wonder they weren't taking it seriously this time around. They'd probably decided it had been just a few lean years, which of course would happen every so often. This year's failure in the apple grove would be considered much the same. "I'll keep that in mind. He's been showing me some of the woods around here. It's a nice area. What else is around here? Any other towns?"

Heinrike seemed to accept that explanation of Ivo spending time with Hansel. He'd have to be more circumspect about meeting up with Hansel, though, to keep suspicion down. At least it seemed like he wouldn't need to worry about the town deciding he was a witch. If he did try to convince them, though, it would be difficult.

"Nothing worth noting," Heinrike said. He shrugged, nodding at Annelie as she came out of the kitchen with a plate of the same stew that she'd served earlier. "There's a small town to the west, Adamore, but they're useless sacks. All they do is whine about being so far away from us and that they never have enough of anything. If they worked half as hard as we did..."

"Heinrike," Annelie said, cutting him off. "Be nice. They were decimated by that illness last year.

And they haven't come to beg in months."

"I guess," Heinrike grumbled, but he did fall quiet. He followed after Annelie when she headed back toward the kitchen, leaving Ivo to eat his dinner in peace. Digging in, Ivo considered his options.

He wasn't going to try and bring up the possibility of a witch to Heinrike, that was obvious. He wouldn't listen. Even if the rest of Surstuhl was more receptive, he wasn't entirely sold on the idea of warning the town. Heinrike aside, it might undermine what Ivo was trying to do.

No, the next step would be to return to the apple grove. He needed to find out what he could from the sigils in the trees, to see if he could pinpoint the witch's location and strength. Then he'd send a letter back to Roesschot, to Alderling. Decided, Ivo finished his dinner quickly and then headed back upstairs to grab his notebook and his jacket.

Outside, Ivo waited for his eyes to adjust to the darkness before walking down the path toward the apple groves. There was no one out this time of night, all the better, but Ivo kept alert just in case. The last thing he needed was someone seeing him do magic. That would end any chance of him taking care of the witch problem in Surstuhl.

He passed Hansel's home as he walked, but he wasn't surprised to see the windows were dark, and there was no sign of anyone inside. Either Hansel wasn't home, or he was already asleep. Probably he was off in the forest, which was understandable. Ivo wouldn't want to sleep in a house he'd shared with his sister if she were missing and potentially dead.

Ivo kept going, slipping into the apple grove,

his footsteps loud in his ears. He made his way through the trees, aiming for a part of the grove that hadn't been touched by the fires. He picked one of the bigger trees and, taking a deep breath, started climbing it. He still hated climbing trees, and luckily he chose correctly, as the tree had one of the softly glowing sigils carved into the trunk.

Settling into the tree's embrace, bracing his feet on a sturdy branch, Ivo simply sat there, listening to his surroundings. It was quiet, the only sound the gentle chirp of crickets and other insects. He still sat for a long while, listening and waiting, but there was no sound, no indication he was anything but alone in the grove.

Setting his hand on top of the sigil, Ivo closed his eyes and loosened his magic. The magic in the sigil was weak, with not as much strength in it as Ivo had expected. He fed it more energy, making the sigil grow brighter as he felt it out. It linked into the others in the grove, as he'd theorized, and from there he was able to follow it. The trail of energy wove through the forest, to the west, past where Ivo thought Adamore was, and deeper into the woods. So west. The magic disappeared there, likely absorbed by the witch, but that was a good starting place.

It wasn't an area Hansel had searched yet, either, if his map was accurate. Ivo disentangled himself from the spell, leaning back in the tree.

A question occurred to Ivo then, and he frowned. Why was the witch pulling energy from the apple grove when she'd already pulled it from the people in Adamore? Why abduct Gretel?

Ivo shook his head. He was missing

something, but he couldn't figure out what. Maybe if they could get close to the witch's cottage, it would fall into place.

The question now was, should he destroy the sigils in the grove or leave them. He'd suggest to Hansel tomorrow that they should search the woods near Adamore, and if he left the sigils in the grove intact that would be one more weapon that the witch could use against them. If he destroyed them, and they didn't find the witch tomorrow, then the witch would have plenty of time to retaliate.

Ivo drummed his fingers against the tree trunk. If he did destroy the sigils, then the witch might get desperate and abduct another of the townsfolk. Or sacrifice Gretel, if she were still alive. He'd leave them, then. The energy the witch got from the grove was miniscule compared to that which a sacrifice would give her, and Ivo didn't want to incite that.

Decided, he started to awkwardly descend from the tree. His feet had barely touched the ground when a shadowy figure stepped out from behind a nearby tree. Ivo drew his knife, alarm screaming through him… but it was only Hansel.

"Didn't expect to see you out here," Hansel said, eyeing the knife but apparently not alarmed by it.

"Couldn't sleep," Ivo replied shortly. He lowered the knife. "You scared a few years off my life there. Ever think about making some noise?"

Hansel snorted, his grin flashing in the dim light of the half moon high above. "Nah. It's my only source of fun, sneaking up on people. What were you doing up there?"

"Looking at the sigil—the witchmark," Ivo said. He shrugged, not sure how much Hansel had seen. Probably not much, just Ivo being weird in the tree. It wasn't as though any of the magic he'd cast was visible. "I can't decide if we should destroy them or not. If we take away this source of power, she might go for a different source, but it might also draw her out."

"She might go for a person," Hansel said, all traces of his smile gone. He sighed, dragging his hands through his hair. "Leave them, then."

Ivo nodded, then asked, "What are you doing out here?"

"Couldn't sleep," Hansel said, repeating Ivo's excuse. He sounded exhausted, but there was no sign of it in his posture. He shrugged, glancing up at the night sky. "I keep thinking about Adamore."

Ivo hummed in agreement. He had too many questions and not enough answers. It was definitely time to write Alderling. "I think we should search around Adamore in the morning. It's more likely her base of operations is nearer there than Surstuhl."

"Probably," Hansel said. "I guess I'll see you at dawn."

"Let's meet at the edge of town, not at the tavern," Ivo said. "I don't think Heinrike likes you."

"Tell me something I don't know," Hansel muttered. "That's fine."

"Good night," Ivo said. Hansel echoed the sentiment, disappearing into the trees as Ivo headed back toward town. Ivo's thoughts were whirling again, but he wasn't going to get anymore answers that night. He'd get some rest, and hopefully tomorrow would be more productive.

*~*~*

Morning came quickly, the sun shining on a bitterly cold day. Ivo munched on a meat-and-vegetable stuffed roll as he waited for Hansel on the western edge of town. He had several more stashed in his jacket pockets, fuel for the day, as he didn't anticipate them returning to Surstuhl until evening.

It seemed colder than Ivo remembered it having been, but winter was only just beginning to sink its teeth into the world. Ivo paced as he ate, partly for warmth and partly so he had a view to each direction Hansel might come from. He finished his roll, and a moment later Hansel appeared—from the woods, of course. Did he sleep out there? How did he keep from freezing? Even a fire would only do so much against the cold.

"Morning," Ivo greeted, approaching. "Ready?"

"As I'll ever be," Hansel said. He didn't look like he'd actually gotten much, if any, sleep. His eyes bore dark circles under them, and his face barely showed any expression. Ivo itched to reassure him, but short of lying he didn't have anything positive to say about the situation.

"Let's go, then," Ivo said. He nodded for Hansel to take the lead. He didn't have a set location on the witch, so there was no point in him trying to find a path through the woods. West of Adamore was the best he'd gotten. Hopefully the search would be successful without them having to camp out in the woods or try again tomorrow.

Hansel was quiet—both in step and in demeanor—as they walked through the wood. Ivo couldn't tell if they were taking the same path they'd taken the previous day to get to Adamore, but they continued generally westerly as they made their way through the wood. Ivo kept an eye out for anything suspicious: signs of magic, signs of people, that eerie calm that had filled the wood before they'd reached Adamore.

"Did you want to visit Adamore again?" Hansel asked after a long while had passed.

"No," Ivo said. He doubted anything had changed. "I see no reason to. Do you?"

"No," Hansel said. He paused, turning toward Ivo. "Do you think they're all dead? Even Gretel?"

"I have no idea," Ivo said, not lying much. He stopped, shrugging. "I've never seen a whole town disappear, and I don't know why a witch would need so much power she'd abduct dozens of people and also put her mark on a grove of trees."

"But they could all be dead," Hansel said.

"They could," Ivo said. "I don't know. It's... the whole thing is odd. I've never seen anything like it before."

Hansel made an unhappy noise, turning to start back through the trees. Ivo sighed, following after him. He wished he had better answers, but it was impossible to tell anything without more information. Something was off about this whole situation, but he couldn't put his finger on it.

They continued to walk, exchanging few

words as they continued through the wood. Hansel seemed to have a plan, not hesitating as he led Ivo through the woods. He changed the direction they traveled every now and again, studying paths and trails through the woods. Ivo trusted him to be a better judge of where they were in the woods and any disturbances than he'd be. Ivo was used to travelling and keeping an eye on his surroundings, but this was different. This wasn't a well-worn path or road.

Until it was.

Ivo frowned at the path cut into the woods, deep wagon wheel tracks scored into the half-frozen mud. This wasn't the road he'd taken to get to Surstuhl. "What road is this?"

"None that I know of," Hansel said. He stepped out of the woods onto it, staring one way, then the other. Ivo followed suit, but the path curved out of sight both ways, hidden by trees and overgrowth.

"Not the loggers?" Ivo asked, but he knew the answer to that. Anything the loggers did would be wider and better reinforced.

"No, they work to the south of Surstuhl, sometimes more east. They wouldn't bother coming this far out," Hansel said. He gestured off to their right. "Adamore is back that way. If I have my bearings, this road should lead there."

"Did you notice a path leading out of town?" Ivo asked. "I didn't, but I wasn't looking for that."

"I wasn't either," Hansel said. His brow furrowed. "Do you think..."

"Well, it goes somewhere," Ivo said. "Maybe all it does is meet up with the main road."

"Maybe," Hansel said, but he didn't sound very sure of that. He scrubbed a hand through his hair, then set his jaw. "Let's go."

Ivo nodded, following after Hansel as he headed down the track. They walked for a while, the woods not changing around them. Oddly, the track showed only wagon wheels; there were no footprints or the tracks of any animals that might have been pulling the wagon. Ivo slowed his steps, wondering if the rain had washed away those tracks, or if the wagon had only left those grooves because it had been carrying a lot of weight.

Such as the weight of a town full of people.

Probably not all at once, of course, but if they were right, and this trail led to the witch's cottage, then this was likely the path between it and Adamore. But how did a single woman, witch or no, move so many people? People were heavy. It wouldn't have been like moving bedding.

"What if there's more than one witch?" Ivo asked, breaking the quiet.

Hansel stopped and turned to stare at Ivo. "More than one?"

"It would make sense," Ivo said, dread creeping into his chest. "Why would one witch need so many people? Why would she need the grove? But what if there's two? I can't imagine there's three or more, or else Surstuhl would have been seeing more effects of the magic. The spells in the grove are amateur. They keep overloading and setting the trees on fire. What if there's a master witch teaching an apprentice her black magic?"

Hansel scowled. "Then we kill them both."

"If we can," Ivo said. He started walking again. "Best to find out what we're facing."

Hansel grunted and followed him. The further they walked, the more Ivo got the creeping sense that something was wrong. It was like the previous day, when they'd approached Adamore, and Ivo was fairly certain that was a sign they were heading in the right direction. They turned another slow curve in the road and Hansel came to a dead stop, staring at a tree.

To be fair, it was a very odd tree. It was nearly pure white versus the regular brown of its neighbors. The trunk was barely the span of one of Ivo's fists. Its branches were nearly perpendicular to the trunk, jutting out in all directions, and it stood half as tall as the other trees.

"I know that tree," Hansel said hoarsely. "It's the same as when we were younger. This is it. This is where the witch lives."

# Chapter Seven

"You're sure?" Ivo asked. He stepped closer to Hansel, staring at the odd tree. It didn't seem to be magic, but that didn't mean it wasn't.

"Positive," Hansel said. He didn't move as Ivo approached, but he followed after Ivo when Ivo headed toward the tree.

"Did it do anything?" Ivo asked. "In the past, I mean."

"No," Hansel said. His eyes never wavered from the tree, and Ivo could actually hear his footsteps as they grew closer, a sure sign Hansel's attention had been fully captured by the tree.

Ivo stared at the tree, his eyes seeking out any sign of magical purpose or intent. There was nothing visible. The tree appeared like the others around it: all the leaves fallen from its branches, no grooves in its flaky bark, no marks or glow of sigils.

"It's weird," Ivo said, "but it looks like it's just a tree."

Hansel didn't look convinced, but he turned his attention back to Ivo. He kept the tree in his line of sight as he did so, though. "What now?"

"We find the house," Ivo said. He tried to project a confidence he didn't feel. He wasn't sure what the next step would be after that. Hopefully the witch's home would give them some idea of her weaknesses and he could formulate a real plan.

"It's through there," Hansel said, gesturing to where the trail ended. There was a patch of trees at the end of the road, where Ivo had previously thought the trail curved. He walked closer, frowning, because the trees weren't quite right. They looked like the forest around them... and that was what was odd. They were a replica of the trees, an almost exact copy, and while Ivo's eyes tried to skip past the edges of the opening they were hiding, when he looked more closely, he could see the frayed edges of the illusion.

"That's not a very good spell," Ivo said. "Can you see the spell or see past it?"

"I see it," Hansel said, lowering his voice. "What if she knows we're here?"

"We'll deal with it," Ivo said. He walked toward the illusion, following the path with the wagon wheel tracks carved into it. The closer he got, the more the illusion faded, until he was right next to it and he could see through it entirely. Ivo studied the view before him, his heart hammering despite his attempts to stay calm.

It was a small cottage, shimmering in the weak sunlight that filtered through the trees. Someone had made it look as though it was crusted with jewels and precious metals, though Ivo bet that illusion would break when he got closer. The house looked pristine, small though it was, with clean windows, sharp corners, and a door that was firmly closed and appeared to be made of crystal.

The clearing around the cottage, however, was a mess. There were scraps of wood everywhere—furniture? Ivo frowned. The remnants of the furniture from Adamore, perhaps? Even more odd was the boxes. They almost looked like coffins, lined up along the side of the house to the right. Were there bodies in there? Ivo didn't want to look, but he would have to eventually.

There was no sign of the witch, though the cabin didn't look abandoned, and something was feeding the glamour. They could wait and see if she appeared, or they could get closer and try to get a better read on the cottage and its potential occupant.

"It's different," Hansel said, his voice barely audible. He'd gotten closer, back to his quiet ways, and Ivo nearly jumped out of his skin when he spoke.

"How?" Ivo asked. Maybe something in the differences could help.

"It looked like candy when I was younger," Hansel said. His brow furrowed, as though he was working hard to remember. "The outside was gingerbread, with sweets on the trim and sugar frosted windows."

"Anything else?" Ivo asked. He edged closer to the nearest large tree, hoping to hide in its shadow.

"Those... crates weren't there," Hansel said. He followed Ivo, eyes barely twitching from the cottage in front of them. "What now? Do you have a special witch trap?"

"Hah," Ivo said. "I wish. No, usually I just overpower them." He sometimes used his magic, and he was unfortunately thinking that he'd have to do that this time. Hopefully Hansel wouldn't react too badly to that. If he were lucky, he could take the witch by surprise and kill her before she was able to react and cast anything. That was supposing there were no traps.

Hansel grunted, not looking particularly impressed by that. Ivo took a deep breath and reached out with his magic, softly feeling out any magic that might be in the area. There was the glamours, on the forest track and the cottage, but past that Ivo couldn't tell. There were no spells on the coffin-boxes, and he couldn't get a read on anything in the cabin past the glamour on the exterior.

"Do you think she's in there?" Ivo asked. He could think of dozens of reasons for the witch to leave: getting supplies for spells, getting more victims for spells, searching out food...

"I have no idea," Hansel said. He shifted impatiently. "Are we going to stand here and stare for the rest of the day? What if Gretel is in there?"

"Then she's probably fine for now," Ivo said. He scuffed around in the dirt by the base of the tree until he came up with a few pebbles. "How's your aim?"

"Perfect," Hansel said, though he looked puzzled when Ivo handed him the stones.

"Throw them. At the door, preferably. One at a time, and we'll see if that draws her out," Ivo said. He tugged the gloves off his hands, not relishing the cold, but if anything did happen, he'd need his dexterity more than he'd need warmth. Drawing both his knives, he nodded to Hansel.

Hansel pitched the first pebble, and it hit the door dead on with a small thump.

Nothing happened.

They waited tensely for a minute, and Ivo

nodded. Hansel threw again, hitting the door again.

Nothing happened.

Hansel threw another pebble.

There was a flicker at one of the windows. Maybe. He wasn't sure; it could have been a trick of the light.

"Again," Ivo said, and Hansel threw again.

"That's all of them," Hansel whispered, looking down to search for more.

"Wait," Ivo whispered back, nudging Hansel's arm with his elbow. There was definitely movement inside, a faint flicker at the window again, as though someone were moving a curtain aside behind the frosted tint. "Did you see that?"

"I think," Hansel muttered. He stared at the house, and they waited tensely for something more to happen.

The door opened. Ivo's breath caught; he hadn't expected to actually lure the witch out, but there she was.

She was elderly in appearance, which struck Ivo as strange. Her hair was gray, short and cut close to her head, spiking around her face. Her face was heavily wrinkled, and she leaned on a cane as she peered about the yard, squinting as though her eyes wouldn't quite focus on things that were further away. She wore a dress that had seen better days, tattered around the hem and patched in several places.

"That is not what I expected," Ivo said softly, but he was talking to air. Hansel was running across the yard at full speed, aiming straight for the witch.

Ivo gaped after him, but then hurried into

motion, knives still at hand. He didn't know what Hansel had planned, but he was sure it wasn't going to end well.

"Where's my sister?" Hansel demanded, then yelped when he seemed to hit a wall abruptly. He fell to the ground, groaning, but almost immediately sprang back up. Ivo paused. That hadn't been a spell in the yard.

The witch laughed, a dry, hoarse cackle. "You should be worried about yourself, boy."

Ivo paused, only a few steps out of the forest. He crept forward, veering off to the right, hoping the witch had bad eyesight and that her focus on Hansel would keep her from noticing his movement.

"What did you do to her?" Hansel demanded. He shoved against the invisible barrier, fury twisting his face.

"What am I going to do with you? You aren't part of the plan," the witch mused, hobbling forward. Her eyes were dark, focused unerringly on Hansel, and Ivo crept closer. She was closer to Hansel than Ivo was to her, but if Hansel could keep her talking, Ivo could probably get close enough to dispatch her without either of them getting hurt.

"Nothing," Hansel snarled. He glanced at Ivo, then took a step back, abruptly stopping when he ran into something else. The witch had him in a box. His eyes widened, and he threw his hands out, hitting the sides of the box. "Let me out of here." Hansel's voice wavered, though he was obviously trying not to let it show.

Ivo hadn't even seen her cast. All the more reason for stealth. Ivo gestured to Hansel, trying to indicate he should keep her talking.

"But you came to me," the witch cooed. "That means I get to keep you. No sharing." The witch's face twisted. "I shan't tell anyone about you." Her gnarled fingers reached out toward Hansel, and she stroked his cheek, reaching through the barrier as though it were nothing.

"Where's my sister?" Hansel demanded again, trying to twist away from the witch's touch. The box appeared to have shrunk, however, and he could barely turn his head away.

"Who knows, by now," the witch said, shrugging. Ivo picked up his pace, and the witch finally seemed to realize he was there, turning. She flung out her hands toward him—and the spell she cast breezed over his skin, the amulet around his neck crumbling as it bore the impact of the spell.

Ivo reached her before her cane hit the ground, plunging his knife into her chest and through her brittle ribs. They snapped under the force of his blow, made brittle by years of spells used to keep them together. She collapsed, a wail dying on her lips, and so did Hansel, falling to his knees as the spell holding him in place broke.

"Oh my gods," Hansel breathed out, pressing his hands against his chest. Ivo leaned down, making sure the witch wasn't breathing and that the knife had gone through her heart. He'd once made the assumption a witch was dead when he hadn't been; that was the last time he wanted to make that mistake.

Putting away his clean knife, Ivo took a deep breath and retrieved the knife buried in the witch's chest. He looked up at Hansel as he cleaned it on the witch's skirt. "Are you all right?"

"Yes," Hansel said, shaking his head. He was shaking, and Ivo walked on his knees over to where Hansel still knelt. He grabbed Hansel by the chin, forcing him to look up. Hansel's eyes were wide, the pupils huge. Spell shock.

"You're suffering the blowback of her spell," Ivo said, tamping down on the urge to chastise Hansel for being so stupid. "Come on, let's move somewhere else and you can collect yourself."

"Into the cottage," Hansel said, not denying he was suffering. "I want to go into the cottage."

"All right," Ivo said. He stood, helping Hansel to his feet. Hansel leaned on him as they walked toward the cottage. The glamour on it had collapsed when the witch had died, leaving behind a ramshackle building that barely appeared to be standing. The roof was full of holes, half the windows were missing, and the walls sagged as though a good wind would blow them over.

Inside wasn't much better. It smelled of death and rot, with dead leaves collected in every corner. There were two tables in the room, both huge and covered with spell accouterments. There were bloodstains on the floor and one of the tables and near a large firepit in the center of the room. A rocking chair sat by the fireside, a dirty, stained knit blanket draped over it, as though the witch had been sitting in it with a blanket in her lap before they'd disturbed her. There was a small bed behind the chair, mussed and covered with several thick blankets.

"Do you want the chair or the bed?" Ivo asked.

Hansel made a face, obviously preferring neither. He was wobbling more, and finally muttered, "Chair."

Ivo got him settled in the chair, throwing the knit blanket onto the bed. Then he fished two of the rolls out of his pockets, handing them to Hansel. "Eat them. You probably don't want to, but do it anyway. It will make you feel better."

Hansel made another face but started to nibble on one of the rolls. "What is this? Blowback? Besides what it sounds like."

"Just what it sounds like. Her spell shattered near you, and the energy blasted you because it couldn't return to her," Ivo said. He prowled the small cottage, but the more he looked, the less it seemed like the witch was worth anything. There were a few animal carcasses thrown roughly in a corner, rotting and repugnant, but there were no signs of human sacrifice.

If it weren't for the missing villagers, Ivo would chalk her up to being a small-time, overly cocky witch.

"Gretel isn't here," Hansel said. He had finished one roll and was just holding the other, staring around the little cottage with a haunted look on his face. "She's probably dead."

"I don't know," Ivo said, replaying what the witch had said. "I don't think this witch killed her. Stay here, eat that roll. You should start to shake it off in a few minutes."

Ivo left before Hansel could protest, immediately heading to the coffin-boxes outside. He wasn't sure what was going on, but if there were bodies in those boxes, he wanted to spare Hansel seeing that, if he could. Ivo quickly approached the first, flipping the lid off and letting it land in the brown grass and dried leaves.

The box was empty. Ivo quickly opened all the other boxes, but they were all empty. Relieved, if confused, Ivo started to head back to the cottage. Hansel appeared before he could reach it, his eyes darting past Ivo to where the empty boxes were lined up.

"Where is everyone? Do you think she buried them?" Hansel asked.

"Not here," Ivo said. He had a theory on what had happened, but he wasn't sure of it. It wasn't anything he'd ever seen. "I don't think she sacrificed anyone, not herself. She was weak, old in appearance. She also said she got to keep you, and that she didn't know where Gretel was. The wagon isn't here."

"You think there's someone else involved," Hansel said. He stepped out of the house, glancing around the yard, his eyes shooting past where the witch's corpse still lay. He grimaced, looking like he might be ill. Ivo shoved his hands in his pockets, checking on his knives. Hansel was an adult; he could manage himself.

"I do. I don't think they're here, though, maybe not anywhere near here. All of this witch's spells were rudimentary. She kept overloading the power spells in the grove, and her glamours here were bad. She also didn't cast many, if any, spells to gain youth. She *looks* old." Ivo rubbed his forehead, the warmth of his face almost startling against the cold of his fingers.

Hansel cursed, storming off. Ivo let him go, staring across the yard toward where the witch lay. What was he going to do now? He'd expected this to end when he'd found the witch or witches. He hadn't expected they wouldn't be nearby. Ivo took a deep breath and headed back into the cottage. Maybe the other witch had left some sort of clue as to who and where they were.

The cottage smelled as bad as Ivo remembered, but he braced himself, choosing to look through the things on the tables first. Everything seemed normal, for a witch. There were dead animals, bits of moss and mushrooms and berries. There were several bowls with foul-smelling concoctions, but no indications on what they were supposed to do.

There were papers, and Ivo picked those up, thumbing through them. They were written in a neat hand, detailed descriptions of easy spells to extend life and gain more energy. They grew slightly more complex, and very specific, as Ivo paged through them. There were directions on how best to lay out the spell web in the grove to draw energy for it, specifically referencing trees at several points throughout the grove.

The last sheet of paper detailed the spells that needed to be cast in Adamore. Ivo stared at the page, reading over it several times. The spells were meant to make the people inside their homes sleep for three days. The witch was to do it on a specific day, some three months prior, and also try to get the drop on 'that nosy hunter woman' who kept stumbling across their spells in the woods.

Then the writer of the notes would show up and help the witch move all the people to some unknown destination, with a reward of youth forthcoming when the townsfolk reached their destination, enough to make her thirty years younger.

Ivo folded the pages and tucked them in one of his coat pockets. He needed to talk to Alderling. There was something bigger afoot here than a simple witch taking up residence in a small town. No, someone had made a witch and stolen nearly two dozen people. Including, possibly, Hansel's sister. Ivo didn't know if getting the drop on Gretel—because who else could 'that nosy hunter woman' mean?— meant killing her or including her in the people who had been abducted from Adamore.

If Hansel hadn't found her, though, Ivo was willing to bet it was the latter. Why waste a perfectly healthy young woman?

Ivo spent several more minutes poking through the rest of the cottage, but he didn't find anything else useful. There were no more notes or letters to the witch or to her mysterious benefactor. All Ivo got was an overwhelming urge to burn the place to the ground.

Leaving the cottage, Ivo glanced around for Hansel, hoping he hadn't gone too far. Ivo didn't want to have to return to Surstuhl on his own. He'd probably manage it, but he also didn't feel right leaving Hansel in the woods. Hansel proved it to be an unfounded fear, rounding the corner of the cottage with a dark expression.

"There's more wagon tracks over there." He

gestured back the way he'd come. "I want to follow them."

"Not today," Ivo said. He held up a hand when Hansel started to protest. "They likely go a fair way. We need to rest and regroup. I imagine whoever is behind this took everyone a long distance away, or else they would have done the sacrificing here."

"You don't know that for sure," Hansel said, but his protest was token. He sighed, twisting impatiently as he surveyed the area. "Are you certain those aren't coffins and there's people buried here?"

"There's no sign of it," Ivo said. "No dirt has been disturbed. I don't think this witch particularly cared about burying, either, not if the animal carcasses inside are any indication. I think those were more likely used to transport people. No one is going to want to look in a coffin to see if the occupant is dead or alive." He grimaced, then jerked his head toward the cottage. "I think we should burn this place and then head back to town."

"I'm surprised it didn't burn last time," Hansel muttered, but he walked over to the house, disappearing inside. Ivo heard something break, and a few moments later Hansel returned with bits of the rocking chair, the ends alight with flame. Ivo took one of the sticks. The two of them walked around the cottage, lighting the sagging roof on fire.

Once it was suitably ablaze, they threw the bits of rocking chair inside the house, and then did the same with the coffin boxes. They stayed in the clearing long enough to make sure the fire wasn't going to jump to the trees or spread beyond the cottage, but the ground was plenty damp from the recent rains and the cottage burned without incident.

They left the witch to rot where she was, and Ivo couldn't feel any remorse for that as they headed back to Surstuhl.

# Part II
# The Wider World

# Chapter Eight

"The trail ends here," Hansel said. He scowled as he surveyed the road before them. They'd been following the wagon tracks out of the woods for nearly an entire day, and had finally reached an impasse. The path had reached the Harhan road, which was one of the major north-south roads in the country. Ivo had traveled it to get to Surstuhl, though he was fairly certain the branch of the road he'd taken to get to Surstuhl was further south.

"Well they can't have gone much further," Ivo said. The wagon tracks curved right, indicating that the wagon had headed north. "How do you suppose they were powering the wagon? There's no donkey or horse tracks, and a wagon traveling with nothing to pull it would be very suspicious."

"I don't know." Hansel sighed, scrubbing a hand through his hair. He looked up and down the road. "North?"

"I think so," Ivo said. "Are you all right with going on? I can keep going without—"

"What?" Hansel demanded. "Why wouldn't I keep going? What do you think, I'm going to abandon my sister because the trail got a little harder to follow?"

"You're further from home, and I don't know

how far this will take us," Ivo said, shrugging. He probably could have found a kinder way to ask, but Hansel had been irritable all day, and Ivo had mistakenly thought it was because he'd been getting further and further from Surstuhl.

"I don't care," Hansel snapped. "I care about finding my sister. If it takes me to the ends of the earth, I will find her and find who took her and make them pay."

"All right," Ivo said. He held up his hands as a peace offering. "It was a stupid question. North of here is Wolueik. We can get some more supplies there in case this takes us more than a few days." Ivo had brought his pack, but only out of habit. He hadn't expected to be gone from Surstuhl for more than a few days at most, but it was better to have it and be prepared if they had to camp out overnight.

"I don't have any money," Hansel said, "but I can scavenge what I need as we go."

"I don't doubt that," Ivo said, "but we won't need much. Food, mostly, so we won't have to spend time hunting along the way. Come on, let's keep going. I want to get as far as we can before night falls." If it were summer, they'd have several extra hours of daylight, but winter meant the sun would be setting soon, within the next hour.

They continued down the track, both keeping an eye out to see if any tracks diverged from the Harhan road. Ivo saw nothing more than a stray footstep here and there, and the road itself was hard-packed and showed barely anything in the way of tracks.

Night approached quickly, and to Ivo's

surprise, Hansel was the one who stopped them, pointing to a slight dip in the trees that lined the road. "That's as good a place as any to spend the night."

Ivo nodded, and they made their way over. The ground was firm and cold, and Ivo started gathering the materials for a small fire. It wouldn't do much, but hopefully it would ward off the chill of the night a little. He'd have to share his bedroll with Hansel, or Ivo might wake up to an icicle instead of a travel companion.

Hansel disappeared as Ivo kindled the fire, returning with several thick branches to feed the fire. He disappeared a few more times, building up a stack of firewood, and Ivo set up his bedding and fished out some food that wouldn't require cooking. They might have the time, but Ivo didn't have the patience to actually cook anything. Hansel returned with another armful of branches, setting them with the rest.

"Sit." Ivo directed Hansel to the side of the bedroll, passing him some of the rolls and dried meat he'd pulled out of his bag. "We'll share bedding tonight. For the warmth."

Hansel nodded, tearing into the dried meat first. He stared at the fire thoughtfully, quietly eating. Ivo let him, though he was curious about Hansel. He was fiercely loyal to his sister, brave enough—stupid enough—to approach a witch without hesitation, but past that, Ivo didn't know much about him.

"If you don't mind me asking, where are your parents?" Ivo broke the silence. He remembered as he asked that Hansel had said his father had remarried, and that Heinrike had mentioned something about the stepmother leaving town.

"My mother died giving birth to me," Hansel said, shrugging. "My father died in his sleep about three years ago. The town doctor thought it was his heart but never was sure. What about you? Do you have any family waiting for you?"

"My sister," Ivo said. He bit off a piece of jerky, chewing it thoughtfully. "She's married now, lives in Roesschot with her husband and several children. They're a handful, but I miss them when I'm gone."

"You live there? When you're not hunting witches, that is." Hansel's teeth flashed in the dark, the firelight reflecting off his grin.

"Yes," Ivo said. "In between witch hunts. It's a good city, if too loud sometimes. You only ever live in Surstuhl?"

"No reason to leave," Hansel said. "I mean, Gretel and I talked about it sometimes. Going somewhere bigger, grander, with more things going on. It never happened. Where would we go? The weather's bad this time of year, and we're too busy come spring with the fields and helping out around town that we don't leave."

"It's hard to leave where you grew up," Ivo said. He and Evi had only settled in Roesschot after the witch in their hometown had murdered their parents and other sister. "It was worth it for my sister and I. We moved to Roesschot when I was sixteen and she was fourteen. It might have been better if we'd been older, but we made it work."

"Why did you go?" Hansel asked. Finished

eating, he stretched his fingers out toward the little fire, letting the flames warm his hands.

"Our family was killed by a witch," Ivo said simply. He didn't go into details. Hansel didn't need to know that Ivo's family had been killed by a witch trying to take out the only people in town she thought posed a threat. Ivo and Evi had only escaped because they'd been out hunting. Ivo had spent years wondering if anything would've been different if he and Evi had been home, but it really didn't matter in the end. They hadn't been.

"Ah." Hansel didn't ask for details, thankfully. Ivo finished the last of his meal and polished it off with a bit of water. He passed the skein to Hansel, who drank deeply and then gave it back. Setting it next to his pack, Ivo yawned and moved to settle in.

"I hope you don't mind getting cozy," Ivo said. Hansel shrugged, staring out into the woods.

"I'll stay awake a while longer," Hansel said. "I'm not much for sleeping."

"Suit yourself," Ivo said. He wanted to nag, to drag Hansel into the bedroll with him, but Hansel was an adult, and Ivo had no claim on him. They were men united in a cause, and he didn't doubt Hansel would go his own way after they determined the fate of his sister.

The chill in the air made it near impossible, but Ivo eventually drifted into an uneasy sleep. He stirred when Hansel joined him at some point later, settling into a deeper sleep with the added warmth, but when he woke, Hansel was gone.

Ivo shook the hair out of his face and stared around the little camp. The fire was still going, which surprised him, but it also meant that Hansel couldn't have gone far. Probably went to piss. Ivo stood up slowly, stretching and willing the aches and pains from sleeping on the ground to disappear. He wasn't that old yet, barely thirty if a day.

Hansel appeared as Ivo finished rolling up the bedding, looking a little rumpled. He nodded in greeting, then stared out at the road. Ivo left him to his contemplation, fishing out more of the same fare they'd eaten the previous night. He passed some to Hansel, who took it even as he started to bank the fire.

"Do you suppose we'll get anywhere today?" Hansel asked as they walked toward Harhan road.

"I hope so," Ivo said. He very much hoped they were able to find where the wagon diverged from the path. He was just guessing that the wagon and its occupants couldn't have gone far, but what if they had? The spells in Adamore had been to put the townsfolk asleep for three days, but the witch who'd taken them could have easily recast that if needed. "If we don't find anything before we hit Wolueik, we can ask around there. Maybe someone will have seen something. It would be hard to miss a wagon full of crates the size of people."

"You would think," Hansel muttered. He ran a hand through his hair, starting north again. Ivo followed, falling into step beside him. "People can be very blind to what's in front of them."

"Surstuhl won't have any further issues from that witch," Ivo said. He almost didn't ask, but he was curious. "Was that the same witch as the one who had you and Gretel?"

"No," Hansel said. He shook his head sharply. "She was different. I shouldn't have reacted the way I did."

"No," Ivo agreed. He'd planned to bring it up, given that it was likely they'd run into another witch, but Hansel hadn't seemed open to conversation the previous day. "We managed, she's dead, and you're alive. That's what we wanted. Next time don't rush the witch, though; we're lucky she was inexperienced. Usually unless you have magic, you'll wind up dead."

Hansel snorted. "I'm no witch. How far to Wolueik?"

"We should be there late tomorrow if I remember correctly," Ivo said. He scanned the underbrush, but like usual, there were no signs of a wagon veering off the road. "I'm surprised you haven't been. Surely Surstuhl has needed something from Wolueik on occasion."

"I never needed to go. Mostly the loggers take trips out there to sell their wood. Occasionally if the town needs something special, we'll go for that, but I was never part of those trips," Hansel said. He was quiet a moment, then asked, "Where do you get your orders from? You mentioned that you were told there were spells being cast around Surstuhl, but you didn't know what they were."

"My superiors work for a branch of the King's Army," Ivo said. "I'm... their employee, I guess you would say. Not technically a soldier, and I can turn down these assignments if I want."

"You can do that? Not enlist, I mean, and still work for them." Hansel looked thoughtful. "Can anyone do that?"

"Not everyone, but some people. Do you want to become a witch hunter?" Ivo asked. It wasn't a bad thought. Hansel obviously had the passion for it, and he might even have the patience for it if his sister weren't involved. Ivo wondered what she'd think of it, whether she'd be part of that if they found her alive.

"Maybe," Hansel said. He shrugged, his mouth twisting angrily. "I don't like the idea of staying in Surstuhl, especially after no one took me seriously about the threat. If they had, maybe we would have found Gretel by now, or realized there was something wrong sooner."

Ivo hummed thoughtfully. He hadn't been there, so he couldn't say what the people of Surstuhl had been thinking. It was easy enough to speculate, but most small towns tended to react much the same as Surstuhl had. "They were scared. If you do decide to pursue it, you'll find that everywhere. People don't like to believe there's a magic problem, because they can't fix that. If it's a harvest issue, or someone running off to another town, that's a problem that can be solved or not a problem at all."

"I guess," Hansel said. "I don't think there's anything to be gained by pretending a problem doesn't exist."

"You'd also have to be careful about stating your intentions," Ivo said. He didn't know if Hansel would heed any of his advice, but maybe he'd be smarter than Ivo and not have to make the mistakes to learn from them. "I've had towns turn on me, thinking I'm the problem because I'm new in town and a stranger, and it's easier to blame me than to accept that someone they'd known all their lives had turned to black magic."

"I can see that. Especially in a town like Surstuhl, where we don't get travelers often."

"Exactly," Ivo said.

They lapsed into a comfortable silence, picking up the pace as the sun rose. The road continued to be deserted—not unusual this time of year, and so far from the major cities—and there continued to be no sign of the wagon changing direction. There was the occasional wheel mark on Harhan road that made Ivo think they were still on the right path, but it was just as possible the witch had driven off into the woods and masked their trail.

After stopping briefly for lunch, they got back on the road. Ivo shared several stories of witch hunting with Hansel, carefully leaving out any mention of magic, and elicited several stories from Hansel, mostly about the tricks he and Gretel had played on their father and the other unsuspecting townsfolk over the years. Apparently, very few people believed the two of them capable of the tricks because they were so quiet and studious otherwise.

Dark fell before Ivo knew it, and they made camp again at the side of the road. The next day passed much the same, though Hansel grew noticeably quieter the further they went without spotting any sort of trail. They reached Wolueik just after dark fell, slipping through the gates before they were closed against the wildlife and any bandits that might have been lurking past the small city's walls.

The street lamps were already lit along the center pathways, and Hansel stuck close to Ivo as they made their way through town, his gaze darting around. If he'd never left Surstuhl, Wolueik would seem huge. Ivo wanted to bring him to Roesschot, just to see his eyes bug out.

"Wolueik is a small city," Ivo said as he headed for the center of town where there were several inns to choose from. "I've been here before, and there's some good folk around. We can get some information and hopefully get a better direction to head in tomorrow."

"I hope so," Hansel muttered. "This is small?"

Ivo laughed, flashing a smile over his shoulder. "Yes. There's plenty of cities much bigger out there. Roesschot is huge, probably twenty times the size of Wolueik. I still get lost there if I wander into the wrong borough."

"Ugh," Hansel said, but he didn't seem entirely put out. Ivo headed toward the inn he'd stayed at the last time he'd been in town. It had good food, decent beds, and wasn't going to empty his coin purse.

"I can't pay you back for any of this," Hansel said as they approached the inn. "I was telling the truth yesterday when I said I have no coin."

"I didn't ask you to spend anything," Ivo said. "I get plenty enough money to fund these trips, so don't worry about it. One more body in an inn room isn't going to cost that much extra, and your help getting around Surstuhl and finding the witch has more than paid for itself."

"If you say so," Hansel said, sounding unconvinced. Ivo didn't push it, heading into the inn. He'd arrange for a room, maybe a bath, and definitely hot food. In the morning, they could see about supplies and track down any leads they could as to where the witch may have taken their captives.

Inside, the inn was busier than Ivo expected. As he remembered from his last visit, two-thirds of the main floor was given over to tables that were crushed in as tightly as possible. Several servers came from the right side of the room, where a massive cooking fire heated the room and also heated the large cookpots that rested mostly in it. There was a second story with the rooms that were let, and the staircase that led to it was tucked into the corner behind the cooking fire.

Ivo headed toward the woman he knew owned the inn, a stout woman who was stirring the biggest pot of food with a large wooden spoon. The shirt she wore had no sleeves, and she had a heavily stained apron covering her trousers and shirt. Ivo nodded, waiting until he was closer to her before speaking.

"Hail, Luzia," Ivo said. He hefted his pack, glancing briefly behind him to make sure Hansel had followed. "I'm in need of two bunks. At least for tonight, maybe for tomorrow."

"I don't have any," Luzia said. Wiping her brow with a corner of her apron, she gestured at the room. "The Winter Revival is starting in two days, and every place in town is full up. The only thing I've got is a single room, and I've only got that because the idiot who was going to rent it from me lost all his coin in a card game."

"How much?" Ivo asked. "I'll pay up front."

"That's why I like you, Ivo. More sense than

most of the lot that come through here. One silver a night. One and a half for both nights, since you're paying up front."

"Done," Ivo said. Luzia included meals with that, and there was a communal bath not far from here if they ended up having time for a bath. "Thanks, Luzia."

Luzia tucked away the coins Ivo passed over, then waved over one of her servers. "Minna, take them upstairs to the empty room. Would you like dinner? Or have you eaten?"

"Food would be wonderful," Ivo said. He eyed the pots appreciatively. Luzia's cooking was more than worth the slightly higher prices she charged for her beds.

"I'll have Minna bring you something once you're settled. The room's full now, but you can eat upstairs, just don't make a mess."

"We'll be neat," Ivo promised.

Minna gestured for them to follow her, heading toward the staircase. She was quiet as she led them upstairs. The little room she brought them to was probably not worth the price Ivo had paid for it, barely wide enough for him to stretch his arms out without touching the walls. There was a small window above the solitary bed, though at least the bed looked large enough to accommodate both him and Hansel. Minna disappeared before Ivo could thank her, shutting the door behind her before presumably going back downstairs to resume her duties.

"Do you think we'll be able to find her?" Hansel asked. He set his pack down on the floor at the foot of the bed and sat down heavily on it. The bed was the only piece of furniture in the room, and Ivo followed Hansel's example and set his bag down on the floor.

"Maybe," Ivo said. "Won't know until we try." He yawned, his jaw cracking with the effort. "We'll find out in the morning. There's plenty of people to ask, and a wagon full of crates of that shape and size would certainly attract attention."

Hansel hummed, though he didn't seem convinced. Ivo wasn't certain they would either, but he wouldn't tell that to Hansel. It seemed unlikely the witch they were hunting would go through a town as big as Wolueik, and even if they had, there was no guarantee they hadn't cast a spell on the wagon to make it appear harmless.

Never mind the Winter Revival festival would mean all kinds of strange wagons and things that were typically out of the ordinary for Wolueik.

Ivo shoved those thoughts out of his head, moving to open the door when someone knocked. It was Minna, back with their supper, which she handed off silently before disappearing again. Ivo passed a dish to Hansel and sat down beside him, tucking in and shoving his worries to the side. Tonight, they'd rest; tomorrow was soon enough to continue tracking down the witch.

# Chapter Nine

Ivo woke entirely warmer and cozier than he could remember being in a long time. For a moment, he reveled in being warm and comfortable, the press of a familiar body next to his... and then he recalled that it was too familiar for the brief period of time he'd spent with Hansel. Waking, he shifted away, wondering how his limbs had come to be so entangled with Hansel's.

It had been a long time since he'd shared a bed with anyone. When he'd traveled with his sister, they'd only shared bedding when it was cold outside. Otherwise they split who slept on the floor and who on the bed.

With the tiny inn room, there hadn't been room to do that without the danger of one of them being stepped on in the middle of the night if the other had to use the washroom. Besides which, he and Hansel had shared bedding on the trip here. Why was it so different to do so when there was a bed?

Ivo didn't know, but it only made him ache with loneliness and highlighted that he was on his own again. Maybe it was time to give up witch hunting and settle in Roesschot with his sister. He could fill his free hours with his sister's children and maybe even spend some time with Evi.

Shifting slowly so that he didn't wake Hansel, Ivo edged out of bed. Hansel stirred but stayed asleep. He looked tired even as he slept, but also younger than he usually did, more innocent and like he needed protection. Ivo rubbed at his face tiredly. He needed to wake up before he did more than think stupid thoughts. Hansel was capable of taking care of himself, even if he'd let his temper get the better of him when they were dealing with the witch near Adamore.

Ivo desperately hoped those people were still alive.

Creeping over to his pack, Ivo settled on the floor and dug out the wax-coated packet that held the paper and envelopes he used to send reports. He dug out a pencil and set to work writing out what had happened thus far, then folded it, sealed it into an envelope, and tucked it into a pocket to send out later. Maybe Captain Alderling would have some information for him on stranger happenings in the general area around Surstuhl.

Not that it would matter if he and Hansel were able to track down the witch who'd made off with the people in Adamore.

Standing, casting one last look at Hansel tucked up in bed, Ivo pulled on his boots and headed downstairs.

It was slightly less busy than it had been the previous night. Near two-thirds of the squished-together tables were occupied, but Ivo was able to reach Luzia without much hassle. After giving her the letter and a few coins to make sure it got sent out in the weekly post, Ivo accepted a plate of the breakfast she was serving and settled at a table to eat his porridge, sausage, and hot biscuits.

He listened to the room, but most of the chatter was about the upcoming Winter Revival festival. The rest was complaining about people or gossiping about who was doing what (or who) that they weren't supposed to be doing. As he ate, Ivo concocted a story that wouldn't scare away or bring about more gossip.

Hansel joined him when he was almost finished with his meal, accepting a plate of food from Luzia with a quiet thanks as he settled in the seat next to Luzia.

"Luzia, before you go," Ivo said, giving her a smile. "Do you know anything about a caravan of bodies coming through from the south? Hansel lost his sister in a bout of sickness, but the bodies were being brought out this way for some fancy doctor to examine to make sure it wasn't something more serious. She had a family ring that he didn't get a chance to retrieve, so we're trying to track it down."

"Nothing I've heard about," Luzia said. She pursed her lips, glancing at the door. "You might could ask the town guards. They've been on the streets more the last few weeks to keep the festival folk in line."

"It would've been two months back," Hansel said, his mouth full of sausage. "This is delicious."

Luzia beamed. "Thanks. Sweet talker. Guards are still your best bet. That or some of the merchants who set up stalls in the center of town. They'd have to pass through the main street unless they weren't heading back out of town, and I definitely would've heard about it if there were bodies being examined in Wolueik."

"Thanks, Luzia," Ivo said, nodding. "We'll start with the guards, then."

"Sure. If you want more breakfast or coffee, just say." She grinned at Hansel and then headed off to tend the cook fires again.

Ivo lingered over his coffee, idly watching Hansel eat. Hansel ate as though he hadn't had a real meal in months, but given that his sister had been missing for months and he'd all but been living in the woods, that probably wasn't too far off.

"What?" Hansel asked, swallowing the last of his sausage.

"Nothing," Ivo said. He smiled, finishing off his coffee. "Want another helping?"

Hansel shook his head. He chugged down the rest of his coffee and stood. "Let's get going."

Ivo nodded his agreement, and moments later they were on the street. It was bitterly cold again, the sun shining brightly with no sign of clouds, and he shoved his hands into his pockets as they walked.

The main street was wide and well packed, traveled by hundreds of feet each day. With the festival coming up, it was likely closer to thousands, and that wasn't counting the carts, horses, donkeys, and more that used the road. Ivo didn't know what the likelihood was that anyone would remember a strange wagon coming through two months previous, but it was their best bet.

As Luzia suggested, he started by asking the guards. Hansel backed up his story about an heirloom—a ring—that his poor dead sister was wearing without any hesitation. It took them asking four different guards before they got anything more than a shrug.

"Yes, I remember that," the woman said, scrunching her brow. "It was odd, because one of the wagon wheels looked about to fall off, but the driver didn't want to stop. Said he was in a hurry and almost to his destination. I asked about the boxes, but he just said it was goods that couldn't be touched by sunlight. I would've pressed, but my shift was over and the captain gets tetchy when we don't report in on time after shift swap."

"Did you see what direction he was going?" Ivo asked. A male witch seemed odd, but it wasn't the oddest thing Ivo had seen or heard of. "Did he mention where he was going?"

"No, sorry. He was headed out of the city, I know that." The guard glanced at the nearby gate that led out of town. "If he wasn't going far, best guess would be Hartsill. It's north of here, a bit to the east. You'd follow Harhan road a ways, and then there's a branch in the road. Harhan continues north, and there's a branch off to the easr that leads to Hartsill. Takes maybe half a day."

"Thanks," Ivo said. "You remember anything else about him? We didn't get to see who took the bodies away."

She shook her head. "It was dark, and he had the hood of his jacket up to ward off the night's cold. If he was carrying sick bodies, it makes sense he wouldn't want to stop and why he was so rude."

"Not a pleasant task," Ivo agreed. He thanked the guard again and headed down the street.

Hansel followed after him, at his shoulder, barely waiting until they were out of earshot before asking, "A male witch? That can't be right."

"Why not?" Ivo asked. He grinned, stifling the urge to flash his magic. That wouldn't end well. "Men can have magic, and there's nothing saying they can't have the same drive for immortality and youth that women have."

"I guess," Hansel said. He didn't sound convinced. "I've never heard of such a thing."

Ivo diplomatically didn't point out that Hansel's experience was limited to a small countryside town. "It happens. Not as often, but it does happen. I've dealt with a few male witches before. But there's nothing saying that this wasn't someone just hired to do a job. We're assuming the driver was a witch, but what if he was just a driver?"

"He's probably dead, then," Hansel said. He sighed, glancing at the sky.

Ivo copied the action. The sun was nearing its noontime high. Should they push on to Hartsill? They had another night booked at the inn here in Wolueik, but they could probably make Hartsill before dark. If the guard's directions were correct; half a day could mean anything from a few hours to several. Ivo could also use some more traveling supplies, especially if he was going to be traveling with Hansel.

"I think we should head to Hartsill tomorrow," Ivo said. "I know you probably want to push on—"

"Tomorrow makes sense," Hansel interrupted. "I do want to get there, to find Gretel, but by the time we're able to leave today, we'd be pushing whether we'd get there before dark. I don't want to stumble on a witch in the dark."

"Exactly," Ivo said, smiling. Hansel returned the smile briefly. "I need to get some more supplies, and I want to ask around some more, see if anyone else has anything to add. Do you want to come with me, or would you prefer to split up?"

"I'll go with you," Hansel said. He smiled again, almost shyly, and Ivo definitely liked that smile more than he should. He was too old for crushes, wasn't he? "I don't have anything else to do, and I want to know whatever you learn."

"All right," Ivo said. He clapped Hansel on the shoulder, and if his hand lingered a moment too long, well, Hansel didn't seem to notice.

*~*~*

Ivo woke to an empty bed, and groaned tiredly as he pulled himself out of the warm blankets Hansel had left behind. Hansel wasn't in the room, so he'd likely gone downstairs for breakfast before they headed to Hartsill. Ivo slowly dragged on his boots and jacket, wishing he had a good excuse to linger in bed. He'd slept poorly, waking up every time Hansel so much as shifted.

The proximity to Hansel was starting to get to Ivo. It didn't help that Hansel was everything Ivo preferred in his men: independent, able to take care of himself, loyal to his family... handsome.

Making a face at himself and his ridiculousness, Ivo made sure everything was settled in his pack and shouldered it, making his way downstairs. Luzia met him at the bottom of the stairs with another plate of hearty food and a steaming cup of coffee, and Ivo crossed the room to the table Hansel had settled at. He was eating more sedately than he had the previous morning, looking thoughtful as he ate.

"Morning," Ivo said, sitting down carefully. He dropped his pack on the floor and started with a long swallow of the hot coffee. It nearly scalded his tongue, but Ivo didn't care.

"Morning," Hansel replied, his brown eyes warm as he studied Ivo. "It tastes better if you don't gulp it down. Saves your tongue too."

"Plenty of people want to see my tongue gone," Ivo said. Mostly witches, but they were mostly dead too. His sister, on occasion, when he wouldn't shut up or said something she didn't like.

"Spite them," Hansel said, grinning as he sipped sedately at his coffee. "That's what I like to do."

Ivo snorted but grinned, amused despite himself. "To be fair, I do end up killing most of the people who want me to shut up."

"That seems extreme," Hansel said. His tone was teasing though, so he definitely hadn't taken Ivo seriously.

"I promise it was appropriate at the time," Ivo said. He dug into his breakfast, trying to ignore the warmth that Hansel's teasing had sparked. Hansel was being friendly, that was all. "You ready for Hartsill?"

"As ready as I ever will be," Hansel said. He sighed, dipping his biscuit into the gravy that covered the remnants of his sausage. "Do you suppose we'll find anything useful there? I can't say I hate the travel, but I would like to... to know."

"We'll find out," Ivo said, trying to be reassuring. He could entirely understand Hansel's frustrations. It was one thing to have his sister missing, presumed dead, but another altogether to be able to confirm it, to accept it and move past it. Ivo certainly hoped she was still alive. "There's so many variables here that I can't tell you for sure. I've never seen anything quite like this situation."

Hansel nodded. He finished off his biscuit, nodding a thanks when Minna appeared to refill his cup of coffee. "How many witches have you hunted?"

Though he'd asked in a low tone, Ivo still glanced around to make sure no one was listening in before answering. "Probably three dozen over the last decade."

"And this is all new?"

"No," Ivo said. "There's aspects of it the same. The energy draw in the apple grove isn't new. That there are multiple witches is, that they took an entire village, instead of one or two or three victims is. The movement of the victims is new..." Ivo shrugged. "But every witch is different, everyone has their own quirks and weaknesses, and almost all of them think they're too good to be brought down. I imagine that's the same here. We'll find out and fix it."

"How did you become a witch hunter?" Hansel asked. Ivo almost choked on his food. Hadn't he answered that the other day? But no, Hansel had asked about his sister, had asked how to become a witch hunter, but Ivo didn't think he'd mentioned his parents.

"I'll tell you when we hit the road," Ivo said. He definitely didn't want to get into it here. Thinking about it was bad enough; if he had to discuss it, he'd probably lose his appetite.

Hansel looked curious, but he didn't push. He drank the rest of his coffee as Ivo finished his breakfast. All too soon, Ivo and Hansel were bidding Luzia farewell and heading out to hit the road to Hartsill.

Ivo waited until they'd left the city, turning the story over in his head. He probably needed to let Hansel know he had magical ability—that technically, he was a witch—but was now the right time to do that? He wasn't sure, so he went the coward's route and decided to omit that piece of his story, even if he also wasn't sure there was ever going to be a right time to tell Hansel. Maybe it would never come up.

"I grew up on the far side of the country, near the coast, in a town that is probably twice the size of Surstuhl. My parents and sisters and I lived in a small house on the edge of town, where it was easy for my parents to gather the herbs and other necessities they needed to make healing poultices and such. They were the town's healers, though they helped with other things," Ivo said. He could still remember running through the fields around town with his sisters, sneaking off to kiss boys in town and trips to the coast to play in the surf during the summer.

He took a deep breath and continued. "When I was sixteen, a witch moved into town. She was... nice, I guess, and fit in easily. She helped out around town without any complaints, was easy-going and hard to anger. Then the strangeness started. My parents figured it out quickly, since they were the healers called when people started getting dizzy, short of breath, tired all the time. They thought it was an illness at first, but no one died.

"I guess she slipped up, though. I don't know what tipped my parents off to the fact that she was casting spells on people and drawing away their life, but they knew. They were talking about how best to confront her, to deal with it, and hadn't decided. The day she killed them, I was away from the house with Evi, off in the fields gathering... something, I can't remember what. I think my parents had sent us on a fool's errand to get us out of the way."

"I'm sorry," Hansel said when Ivo paused.

"It was over a decade ago," Ivo said. It still hurt, but it was a dull pain, an ache for what could have been. He wouldn't have become a witch hunter or traveled the country the way he had, but there was a part of him that thought settling down as a village healer somewhere wouldn't have been a terrible path to take. "She killed my parents and kidnapped my oldest sister, Oda. The whole town was up in arms, but Evi, my other sister, and I were the ones who tracked her down and killed her. She'd already killed Oda, completing the spells she'd been slowly casting on the village women, but she tripped up somewhere and we... were able to kill her."

He'd always remember that fight, the screams, the burn of magic and the way the witch had gone up in smoke when Evi had plunged a knife into her back. Nothing had been quite as shocking since, even if some of the witches he and Evi had killed had had similarly destructive ends.

"So you decided to go hunting other witches after?" Hansel asked. He walked close to Ivo, and Ivo had the urge to lean in, but he squashed that impulse.

"No, not really," Ivo said. "We left home after that, Evi and I. We didn't want to stay in the house our parents had died in. At first, we were going to go home after a year, but we ran into another witch practicing black magic on our travels, and we killed her too. It was there we ran into the King's Army, specifically a Lieutenant Alderling. He was second in command of a branch of the King's Army that deals specifically with stamping out black magic."

"Why they don't just outlaw magic is beyond me," Hansel muttered. He huffed out a sigh. "I guess it wouldn't stop anyone."

"There's plenty of good magic out there," Ivo said softly. "It's more subtle than black magic, is all, and most people don't practice it openly for fear of being mistaken for a practitioner of black magic." Hansel shrugged, and Ivo took that as his cue to continue. "Alderling conscripted Evi and I, but we only agreed to help so long as we didn't need to join the army. He pulled some strings and made that happen. I know he's got a dozen of us who work this way, though I've only ever met one or two of them."

"Did your sister stop?" Hansel asked curiously. "Or do you work separately?"

"She retired, so to speak," Ivo said, grinning. "She met someone, got married, and has children. Lives in Roesschot growing herbs and making potions, just like our parents did."

"She likes it there?" Hansel asked. "Are you returning there after this?"

"She does," Ivo confirmed. "It's too much city for me, most of the time, but I do stay there between trips out. You think you'll go back to Surstuhl?"

"Maybe," Hansel said. He shrugged again, a frown turning his mouth down. "I'm not sure. It's... it won't be the same, even if Gretel is alive."

Ivo nodded in agreement, completely understanding that sentiment. For the first year after he and Evi had left home, nothing had felt right. It was only after traveling for months that he finally found a kind of peace on the road. Perhaps Hansel would find the same.

# Chapter Ten

Hartsill was, as promised, a smaller town off the western side road. It took Ivo and Hansel the entire morning to make the trip to Hartsill, and Ivo took a moment to breathe as they stood in the center of the quiet town. There was almost no one about, and as he looked at the small houses clustering around the square, he noted closed curtains and the way the few people who were out avoided looking at them.

"Something seems off," Hansel said quietly from Ivo's left side. "I don't know what, but there's something."

"I agree," Ivo said. He reached out softly with his magic, feeling things out. There was magic in the town, that much he could tell, but nothing specific and nothing strong nearby. Sighing, he started walking again. "Let's go have a look around town. Maybe we'll run into someone who wants to talk to us."

Hansel nodded his agreement, and they headed deeper into town. A woman scurried into a house further down the road, slamming the door, and Ivo's eyebrows rose. There was busy, and there was just plain antisocial. Why did the town appear to be avoiding them? People disappeared as they approached, and in one instance, a man dragged his child inside and firmly shut the door behind them.

"I really don't like this," Hansel muttered. Ivo nodded, the back of his neck prickling. He glanced around as the houses started thinning out and the forest started to thicken, with more trees and bushes cluttering the space past the road. "Ivo."

Ivo looked to where Hansel was pointing, his other hand tight on Ivo's arm. There was a wagon parked next to a dilapidated cottage, one wheel bent but still attached. In it was a single coffin-shaped box that looked as though it had been cobbled together from bits of leftover and broken furniture.

"Well," Ivo said softly. He reached out with his magic... but there was no magic on the house or in it. There was only a faint touch of it on the box inside the cart. "Let's go, then."

Hansel nodded, letting him take the lead this time instead of rushing forward. Ivo headed toward the cart first to find out what the magic was. The lid of the box was ajar, and Ivo gave it a shove, revealing an empty box. At one end a sigil was carved, one that was similar to the sigils on the houses in Adamore.

"They're spelled to have the occupant 'sleep the sleep of the dead'," Ivo said, keeping his voice low. "So they're unconscious while they're transported."

"That makes sense, but where are the rest of them?" Hansel asked. He looked around again, but there were no other boxes in the area, and there should have been many, many more. There was no signs of a witch here, so likely this was just a pass-through spot, and the activity had spooked the locals enough to be wary of any strangers.

Ivo shook his head. He dropped his pack, made sure his knives were accessible, and stormed over to the front door. He banged on it loudly, Hansel on his heels. Not waiting for an answer, Ivo opened the door, giving it a hard shove when the latch caught.

Inside, a man stood in the middle of the room, brandishing a kitchen knife.

"You get out of here, now, or else!" he shouted, but his voice was anything but steady. "I don't need no trouble!"

"Too late," Ivo said. "Where's the rest of them?"

"Rest o' who?" The man waved his knife. "It don't matter. Out!"

"No," Ivo said. He drew his own knives and prowled forward, approaching the man swiftly. The man squeaked, dropped his knife, and ran for the back door. Ivo caught up to him before he could get to it, grabbing the man by the collar and shoving him toward and then against the wall. Positioning his knife against the man's throat, he smiled darkly.

"You're not a witch, but I'll kill you all the same if I need to," Ivo said, leaning in so his face was inches from the man. "Where are they?"

"I don't know!" The man's eyes were wide, darting frantically around the room as though something or someone might come save him. "I don't, I swear! They just paid me to move the bodies, not to ask questions!"

Ivo leaned back. "Tell me everything, or I'll spill your blood without remorse." He pressed the tip of his knife against the man's throat, letting him feel the cool metal against his skin.

"I will, I will!" The man seemed well enough shaken, so Ivo took his knife away, but kept hold of the man's shirt, not trusting him to not run off.

"Go ahead," Ivo prompted when the man said nothing, only stared at them like they might eat him.

"It wasn't my idea," the man said, wrapping his arms around himself as though he was warding off a chill. "I only did it for the money. Jasper said it would be some quick money, he just needed me to pick up a load and not look too closely at it. Well, I didn't expect it to be from a witch. She nearly killed me!"

"What a loss that would have been," Hansel muttered, making the man's eyes shoot to him.

"So you went to Adamore and picked up people," Ivo prompted. "Then what?"

"I brought them back here. Jasper said to leave them outside in the cart and that would be the end of it, and it was. He took them from there, except he left one of those cursed boxes and didn't give me the money we agreed to, and my wagon's broken now..." The man trailed off, clearly realizing that this was not the audience to expect sympathy from.

"How many?" Ivo asked.

"Twenty? I think, I lost count. We crammed a few in each box. They were all still alive," the man said, spreading his hands. "I didn't hurt them, I swear to it."

"No, you didn't," Ivo said, his anger growing. He'd call the man a weasel, but that would be giving weasels everywhere a bad name. "Where did they get taken to? Where's this Jasper?"

"He was headed north. He said Genkerk, though I don't think I was supposed to hear that. He's got a friend there that will sell them or something." The man shrugged. "That's all I know, I swear."

"When did they leave?" Ivo demanded. "Why do you have an empty box here?"

"Six weeks back, I think. Maybe five." The man shrugged. "I don't know why they left a box; they didn't share it with me. They told me to stay inside. Took my horse too, the ass."

"Was there a young woman, dark hair and a scar on her cheek here?" Hansel asked, gesturing across his cheek. "About my age."

The man hesitated, obviously reluctant to answer, so Ivo gave him a good shake. "Yes! Yes, she was one of them. I'm sorry! I didn't know what it was they wanted me to do!"

"Shut it," Ivo said. He shook the man again. "You're lucky we need to get going and I'm not as bloodthirsty as your ilk. If I find out you've sent any sort of message to warn them we're after them, though, you'll be sorry we left you alive."

Hansel made some sort of noise that looked like he was about to protest leaving the man alive, but Ivo ignored it. He wasn't going to let the man simply carry on, if that was what Hansel was worried about. He shook the man again, then let him go, and the man dropped like a sack of potatoes, blabbering that he wouldn't say a word to no one, no how.

"Let's go," Ivo said. He turned and stalked from the house, Hansel on his heels.

"Are you sure we shouldn't at least wound

him?" Hansel asked, slamming the door behind him. "It feels wrong to just... leave him."

"I'm going to send in the King's Army to pick him up and bring him to a city for a trial," Ivo said. "Once we're at a bigger town, one that has an outpost or mail service."

"Good," Hansel said. He took a deep breath, falling into step as they walked back toward town. "You think the whole town knows?"

"I think the town knows something odd is afoot. I wouldn't doubt there's been several odd men coming and going to that house. They probably think we're to do with it and want to avoid the trouble," Ivo said. "Which is fair. I wouldn't want my family involved in trafficking witch victims."

"Do you think any of them are still alive?" Hansel asked, scrubbing a hand through his hair. "At least he confirmed that Gretel is among them. I mean, I know the witch's notes said..."

"I don't know," Ivo said. He sighed, clapping Hansel on the shoulder and letting his hand rest there. "If she is, we'll do everything we can to find her and get her somewhere safe. The same for the rest of Adamore's citizens."

"Thanks," Hansel said softly, casting Ivo a soft, thankful look that made Ivo's stomach twist in an alarming way. He dropped his hand from Hansel's shoulder, returning his smile.

"Come on, let's get moving. I want to see how far we can get toward Genkerk," Ivo said, picking up the pace.

"How far is that?" Hansel asked, matching his pace without effort. He could probably outpace Ivo, if it came to that.

"At least two days of travel, maybe three? It's along Harhan road, so we'll have to backtrack and then head north again." Ivo had a map that might be useful, but he'd save pulling that out for when they stopped. "I'll look it up when we stop later."

Hansel nodded and fell into step beside him as they left Hartsill behind and headed back toward Harhan road.

*~*~*

Three days later, Ivo was wishing he'd never accepted this mission from Alderling. It had rained almost non-stop the entire trip up to Genkerk, stopping only when that rain had turned frozen and then into snow overnight a few times. He and Hansel had been wet, cold, and miserable when they'd arrived in Genkerk, and things weren't much better now that they were venturing out again.

The sleet fell heavy and hard as they made their way toward the docks, where the innkeeper at their latest inn had said they'd be best suited to find someone transporting bodies. She'd mentioned a healer in particular who was good at containing sickness with her spells, which had made Hansel bristle, but he hadn't said anything then.

"Is a witch casting going to be an issue for you?" Ivo asked. He was walking closer than he technically had to, but the sleet was heavy and cold, and he wanted to be sure he was heard. That was the only reason for his closeness.

Hopefully he was fooling Hansel more than

he was fooling himself with that bad excuse.

Hansel just shrugged. "You think she's the witch we're looking for?"

"If she's not, then she might know who or where we need to go for us to find what we need," Ivo said. Though if she wasn't aware of the wrongdoings going on in her city, then she wasn't much of a witch.

Ivo shook that thought aside. That wasn't fair. There were plenty of reasons she might not have noticed the issue, and he wasn't going to judge her sight unseen.

The docks were as quiet as the streets leading to them had been. There were a few people here and there hurrying from place to place, but no one was lingering, which Ivo didn't blame them for. He wanted nothing more than to be inside, hiding away from the foul weather, but they'd lost enough time on the road already.

About a block from the lake Genkerk sat on was the small building the innkeeper had told them about. It was a short, stout building with a shingle out front that proclaimed the occupant was a healer of small woes, with the witch's name inscribed underneath. *Rosalie von Brandt.*

"This is it," Ivo said loudly. Hansel slowed enough for Ivo to take the lead, which he did, hoping that this would be a good introduction for Hansel to white magic. With luck, he'd learn that it was the caster that was the problem, and not every witch was a black witch. Then maybe Ivo could let it slip that he had magic of his own.

Knocking loudly, Ivo waited as the sleet beat

down on them. His jacket, coated to keep moisture out, was still having a hard time with the mix of ice and rain that it had been inundated with in the last few days.

The door opened after a moment, revealing a slight woman dressed in a thick sweater and trousers that disappeared into thick knitted socks. Nothing she wore matched: the sweater was a bright orange that did not complement the green trousers, and her socks were both different patterns that included several colors.

"Are you Ms. von Brandt?" Ivo asked, giving her a smile.

"I am. Come in." She stepped back, waving them both into what turned out to be a small, cozy room. It likely took up most of the space on the first floor of the building. "If you'll leave your coats and boots by the door to keep the weather contained, I would appreciate it. Have a seat by the fire when you're done. I'll make tea."

With that, she walked across the room to a small doorway that was blocked by a shimmery curtain. A kitchen or something must have been back there, as the sounds of her pottering around were audible, even though Ivo could see nothing past the curtain. Following her instructions, Ivo shucked his jacket and boots, leaving the boots neatly by the door and hanging his jacket on the coat rack.

Hansel did the same, and then they crossed the room to the sofa and chairs set up around the fire. Hansel took a seat close to the roaring fire, eyeing the sigil that glowed in the stones in front of the hearth with suspicion.

"It's to start and feed the fire," Ivo explained. "A simple spell."

"Seems useful," Hansel said. He glanced around the room, his expression going blank, giving Ivo no idea what he was thinking.

To be safe, Ivo reached out with his magic and checked out the spells inside the building. There was nothing untoward; there were plenty of small 'household' spells like the fire spell, and several more that he recognized from his time helping his parents with their shop. If Rosalie von Brandt was casting black magic spells, she was discreet about it.

As if summoned by that thought, she appeared from the back, bearing a large tray that held a teapot in a terribly-knitted cozy, several mismatched tea cups, and several plates of cookies and biscuits. She set the tray on the small table that rested between all the chairs arranged around the fire and then poured them tea.

The whole building seemed to bear her touch of whimsy, from the mismatched tea cups to her clashing wardrobe. The room was filled with knickknacks and knitted bits and bobs of various skill. There were several different colored throws around the room, and the whole place was cluttered, with things on every available surface and then stacked higher in several places. It was homey, though, and despite the discordance, soothing. It felt like his parent's shop, so long ago, even though it only superficially resembled it.

"Eat, please, don't stand on ceremony," Rosalie said. "I'm Rosalie, as you know. What are your names?"

"Ivo," Ivo supplied, and when Hansel didn't immediately reply, he said, "and my companion is Hansel. We're hoping to get your help with a problem we're working on."

"Oh?" Rosalie asked. She picked up one of the cookies, breaking it in half before biting into it. "I take it you're not after a minor spellbreak or a cure for an illness, then?"

"No, unfortunately," Ivo said. He poured himself a cup of tea, adding a small amount of sugar. Hansel didn't move, but if he wanted to sulk and not partake of a warm beverage after they'd been outside again, that was his choice. "We're looking for a witch practicing black magic. I know it's not you—"

"Thank you," Rosalie said, quirking a smile at him. "You're the first witch hunter I've run into that hasn't assumed I'm part of whatever problem they're after."

Hansel shifted restlessly, but Ivo continued, undeterred. "I've known more good witches than bad. Your shop shows no signs that you dabble in black magic, and we do need help."

Rosalie smiled again, finishing her cookie and taking another. "Well, I'll certainly do my best to help you, but my magic is small. I barely have enough power for the little that I do."

Ivo nodded and filled her in on what they were looking for and had run into so far. Rosalie's soft, pleasant expression shifted as he spoke, her brow furrowing and her mouth turning down in worry as he described the way the entire town of Adamore had been kidnapped.

"That's troubling," Rosalie said. "I've never

heard of such a thing. A person or two, certainly. Everyone knows the stories of witches kidnapping women and children for power, but an entire town? And then moving them so far..." She shook her head. "I don't know how I can help, though. I haven't seen anything..." She paused, her brow furrowing. "No, that's not quite true. Well, it is and it isn't. I didn't see anything, but I did have a strange feeling..."

"Oh?" Ivo asked. As weak a witch as Rosalie was, a feeling was likely all she'd have gotten if she'd passed by a spell cast using black magic. "Where?"

"I can show you. If you're up to it? The weather is atrocious, and I know you've both been traveling hard," Rosalie said.

"Show us," Hansel said, the first words he'd spoken since they'd entered the building. He paused, seeming to realize how rude that sounded. "Please."

Rosalie smiled at him sweetly. "Absolutely. Let me go find weather-appropriate clothing." She stood up and crossed the room, disappearing behind the curtain again. A moment later, they could hear footsteps above them, so whatever loft space the building had was accessible from the back.

"She's... not what I expected," Hansel said quietly. He folded his hands together, his eyes on the curtain where Rosalie had disappeared. "You're sure she's honest?"

"Yes," Ivo said. He was sure, even if he couldn't explain to Hansel how he knew that. Hopefully he'd just take it that Ivo had experience with witches and would leave it at that. Hansel nodded, falling quiet again. Ivo helped himself to a few more of the biscuits, chasing it with tea. Hansel hadn't touched the food or tea, but Ivo didn't nag him about it. Hansel was an adult; if he wanted to eat, he would.

Rosalie reappeared after a moment, wearing a less bulky sweater, a jacket pulled on over it that looked as though it had been coated like Ivo's had to help prevent water from soaking into it. She wore a pair of boots that laced up the front and reached her knees, and had pulled her short brown hair under a thick cap.

"Shall we?" She asked.

A few minutes later, boots and jackets back in place, the three of them hit the streets. Rosalie led the way, seemingly barely hindered by the sleet that still fell or the slush and slickness they slogged through as they headed further down the docks. The buildings slowly turned from well-tended and neat to unkempt, from respectable to disreputable. There was almost no one about, everyone tucked inside still, and hopefully that was to their benefit.

Several minutes later, Rosalie stopped, frowning at the buildings that lined the street around them. None of them were in great shape; several were missing windows, letting the elements in, and several more had boarded up doors and windows.

"Here," Rosalie said. "Here is where I get that weird feeling."

# Chapter Eleven

Ivo reached out his magic to feel around the area, and as he expected, Rosalie was right. There was a nasty spell very close. He eyed the nearby buildings before deciding it was probably the one with the boarded up windows and doors next to the building they'd stopped in front of. It looked as though it had been a warehouse at one point, though he doubted it served that purpose any longer.

"Let's look there," Ivo said, gesturing to the building. "Rosalie, if you'd like to go back—"

"No," Rosalie said simply. She smiled at them both, gesturing for Ivo to lead the way. "You first, witch hunter."

Ivo snorted but led the way, Hansel close on his heels. Rosalie followed at a more sedate pace. There was no clear way to get inside from the front, so Ivo walked around the building, scouring the outside as best he could for sigils or any sign of a way in. Between the darkening sky and the rain, it was entirely possible he had missed a sigil.

Around the back, there was a doorway that looked to be in better repair than the rest of the building. Ivo headed toward it, his steps squelching in the half-frozen slush behind the building. Hansel stayed close, Rosalie a step or two behind them. The door was firmly shut, and Ivo inspected the door frame, almost missing the sigil carved into the door beneath the handle.

It seemed familiar, but Ivo couldn't place it. Something about it rubbed him the wrong way, though that could simply be the circumstances of where they'd found it.

"What do you make of this?" He gestured to the sigil, and Rosalie stepped in, leaning close to peer at it. She hummed softly, the sound barely audible over the sleet falling.

"I think it's a protection charm," she said. Her words sparked the recognition in his mind, and he yanked her away from the door as she reached out to touch it.

Too late—the sigil exploded with enough force to send them both tumbling to the ground. Ivo tried to take the brunt of the fall, curling around Rosalie. He hit the ground with enough force to knock the wind from him, his head spinning. That wasn't a protection charm. It was a trap charm. He'd seen one of those before, years ago, during one of the first witch hunts he'd done.

"Ow," Ivo grumbled, sitting up and letting Rosalie go. He looked to Hansel, relieved to find him still standing. He was several steps away, his brow furrowed and his stance suggesting he was about to attack someone.

"Well, I wasn't expecting that," Rosalie said with a shaky laugh. Ivo helped her sit up, then climbed to his feet and helped her stand. She smiled at him, though it didn't quite reach her eyes.

"Are you all right?" Ivo asked. "We can

proceed without you." It would probably be safer for her, given she wasn't strong magically and had nothing invested yet.

"No, I'll be fine," Rosalie said. She mustered another smile, leaning into him for a brief second before stepping away.

Ivo turned to Hansel, surprised to see his expression a thundercloud. He hadn't seemed that angry before. Did he think Rosalie had exploded the sigil on purpose? "Are you all right, Hansel?"

"Fine," Hansel said shortly. He turned sharply on his heel and stalked into the building, and Ivo shook his head. His doubts about telling Hansel about his magic weren't being soothed. He sighed, following after and making sure Rosalie followed him. Inside, the building was dark, with only the barest hints of gray light peeking through some of the gaps in the windows.

Hansel hadn't gone more than a few steps into the building, so they caught up to him quickly. Rosalie shifted behind them, muttering something, and Ivo winced when light flared into existence.

"Too bright, sorry!" Rosalie said, turning away and hiding whatever light she'd conjured from them. She muttered several more words, and the light dimmed slightly. "How's that?"

"Perfect," Ivo said. The light cast shadows across the warehouse's floor, highlighting fallen beams and cobwebs in near every corner.

They were in the right place, that much was immediately clear. There were several empty coffin-shaped boxes on the far side of the room, near where the front door was. There was also a large wagon, large enough that it could easily have carried twice the number of people from Adamore. Ivo reached out with his magic, immediately finding several spells on the boxes.

Were there people in them?

That would wait. There was another spell, a nastier spell, and Ivo walked toward it slowly. Rosalie and Hansel followed, the sound of their footsteps echoing through the mostly empty room.

"There's a glamour," Rosalie said. She eyed Ivo with curiosity, but if she suspected Ivo had magic, she didn't say or ask. "Hold this." She passed the light to Hansel, whose expression was still unhappy. He fumbled the ball of light briefly before awkwardly holding it. Rosalie reached out a hand toward the place where the glamour was and said, "You may want to take a step back. I don't do this often."

Ivo didn't move, not concerned. Breaking a glamour wouldn't produce anything as explosive as setting off the door trap, not unless Rosalie did it extremely poorly. When she didn't immediately move to break the spell, Ivo prompted her. "Go on."

"If you're sure." She glanced at Hansel, but Hansel said nothing, his face still a thundercloud.

"We're sure," Ivo said. Rosalie nodded, then grimaced. She muttered a few words, then shook her head and said something else. The glamour wavered, and then snapped, the fake image disappearing. Where before they could only see empty warehouse was now a filled room. There were several more crates and barrels visible, in much better repair than those that had come from Adamore.

Behind one of the barrels was a foot. Ivo frowned, walking toward it. As he walked, the foot retracted, hiding behind the barrel. Hansel fell into step behind him, though Rosalie seemed content to stay where she was. Ivo rounded the side of the barrel, tensed for whatever might come.

There was a man behind the barrel, hunched down, and Ivo's first thought was that he was one of the victims, maybe from Adamore or maybe from somewhere else.

Then the man snarled at him and shoved away from the wall he was leaning against, lunging at Ivo with his hands outstretched, curved into claws. Ivo took a step back, but Hansel was there before he could do more than that, tackling the man from the side and forcing him to the ground. The man twisted and shrieked, snarling epithets and insults that were barely comprehensible.

Hansel wrestled with him a moment, and as Ivo was stepping forward to try and help subdue the man, punched him hard in the jaw.

The man sagged with a cry, finally stilling, though he glared hatefully up at Hansel as though he was the source of all of the man's woes.

To be fair, he was the current problem.

"Who are you?" Ivo demanded. Hansel slowly got off the man, standing over him menacingly. Ivo stepped up to join in, crossing his arms and staring down at the man.

The man shook his head, mimicking Ivo by crossing his arms. He flopped back against the stone floor, seemingly oblivious to the way his head cracked against the stone, and shut his eyes.

Hansel nudged his leg with the tip of his boot. "Answer the question."

"Nope, nuh-uh," the man said, shaking his head. "I'm not here, you can't see me, I'm not here."

"Try again," Ivo said. "Who are you and why were you hiding behind a glamour?"

The man twisted, opening his eyes to glare hatefully at Ivo. "You've ruined it! You've ruined it all! Now she's going to come and take me too, and no one will see me ever again."

"Who?" Ivo asked. "If we can get to her first—"

The man barked a despairing laugh. "You'll never find her. She is only found when she wants to be found. You'll never find her. You shouldn't be able to see me."

"We can, though, so we can find her too," Hansel said. His tone was softer. Maybe he thought he could get something out of the man with a nicer approach. "What are you doing in here?"

"Doing..." the man sat up, pointing to the barrel. "You can find her? She doesn't like to be found. She likes to be sent her people, but she doesn't like to come here. It's cold, she says, and it smells." He shook his head vigorously. "It doesn't smell. You don't think it smells, do you?"

"It doesn't," Ivo said. He didn't smell anything too bad, it was true. Nothing he wouldn't expect in a decrepit warehouse with a strange squatter in it. "What do you do here?"

"I make things." The man pointed to the barrel again. "Smaller things for holding people. Less... like they are going to a funeral." Hansel tensed beside Ivo, but he didn't make any move.

"When was the last time you had people here?" Ivo asked. He looked more thoroughly at the things that had been hidden behind the glamour. The crates and barrels did look as though they'd be big enough to fit a full-sized adult. It certainly wouldn't be comfortable, though Ivo doubted that was the point of the exercise.

"There's always people here. I'm always here." The man shuffled sideways, glancing over Ivo's shoulder to where Rosalie stood. "Put it back, please, can you put it back?"

"I can't, I'm sorry," Rosalie said. She offered the man a smile. "What's your name?"

"Lors, I'm Lors," he said, frowning at her. "She won't like it if you don't put it back. She'll be mad."

"When will she be back?" Hansel asked. "We can explain to her, make sure she's not mad at you."

"She's always mad at me," Lors said, shaking his head. "She doesn't say she's coming, she just comes."

Hansel glanced at Ivo, frowning. "I don't like this."

"I haven't liked any of this since Surstuhl," Ivo muttered. He frowned at Lors, wondering what to do with him. He obviously wasn't entirely sound of mind, and whoever he was working with had manipulated him into helping. "Do you move the people?"

"I move the people from their boxes to these boxes," Lors said. He stood suddenly, scrambling up and over to one of the barrels. "Like this."

Ivo walked over, keeping a cautious eye on Lors as he looked in the barrel. There was a spell on it, that much was clear the moment he got a look at the contents. There was a body inside, obviously long dead. A man, to judge by the little Ivo could see of his clothing and hairstyle. His skin was sunken and he looked mummified, his features distorted beyond all recognition. The spell on the barrel must have been to keep the smell inside, as there was absolutely no way the body didn't smell.

"How many of your boxes have people now?" Ivo asked. He almost didn't want to know, but he needed to know. Did the witch kill them here? Or did she simply store the bodies here? There were almost a dozen barrels and crates in the area where Lors had been working.

"This one, that one," Lors said, gesturing to a crate close to Hansel. Hansel grimaced, but walked over and opened the top. His expression hardened when he looked inside. Only two bodies... that wasn't a lot, given more than two dozen people had lived in Adamore.

"When did you last see her?" Ivo asked, but Lors only shrugged. He walked over to a pallet that was tucked in the corner, sitting down on it and glancing woefully around the room.

Frowning, Ivo left him be. He gestured to Hansel, and together they checked the other crates and barrels. As Lors had said, however, they were all empty. Only the two had bodies. Both men, Ivo ascertained after a whispered conversation with Hansel. They rejoined Rosalie, who was inspecting the barrel with the body that Ivo had found.

"This is the spell I could feel," Rosalie said. Her eyes flickered over to Lors briefly, but he hadn't moved from his pallet, sitting on the edge of it and picking at the blanket on top of it. "It's keeping the body from rotting and basically... keeping it enclosed in this space."

"Which is why it doesn't smell," Ivo said. "Ugh." He shifted his weight, considering what to do next. "Is there a King's Army outpost here?"

"Yes, a small one," Rosalie said. "You want to turn this over to them?"

"At least this," Ivo said. He jerked his head slightly toward Lors. He lowered his voice. "Him. I don't think we'll be able to get more information out of him, and we definitely can't leave him on his own."

"All right," Rosalie said. "I can go fetch them, if you two want to stay here. Or I can give one of you directions and stay here with the other."

"Go ahead and go, if you think you'll be safe," Ivo said. "I want to look around a little more before we turn this over to the King's Army."

"I'll be fine," Rosalie said. She grinned at him, picking up the light that had fallen from Hansel's hands. "Here, you take this."

Ivo nearly fumbled it when she threw the spell to him. He hadn't done much in the way of magical transfers, but a light spell was easy enough. The light faded slightly and then flared brighter until Ivo modulated it.

Rosalie's grin widened, but all she said was, "See you in a bit." How she'd guessed he had magic was beyond him, but at least she hadn't said it. Ivo still wasn't sure how Hansel would react.

"Come on, let's look around," Ivo said. Rosalie slipped out the back, and Ivo and Hansel started poking around the warehouse. Hansel kept close to Ivo, and they both kept shooting looks at Lors, making sure he wasn't about to try anything or make a break for it.

They poked around the rest of the warehouse, but there was no further magic. The coffin-shaped boxes on the far side of the warehouse bore the same marks as the ones at the witch's cottage west of Adamore, to keep their occupants asleep, but nothing else. Several of the boxes were missing pieces, either re-purposed for Lors's barrels and crates or burned for warmth. There was a small fire pit near where Lors sat, but no fire currently burned.

"What do we do now?" Hansel asked. They'd looked in near every corner of the warehouse, but nothing had turned up. "Lors is not Jasper, and there's no clues as to where any of the rest of the people from Adamore went."

"We could stake out this warehouse," Ivo said. That was a last resort, as he didn't think it would net them anything. The witch would know her spells were broken and avoid coming here. There was nothing to draw her in; she'd call it a loss and move on. "That probably won't help, though. Maybe the King's Army here knows something more or can give us a direction to go in."

"I hope so," Hansel muttered. He frowned at the barrels, moving to inspect them again. Ivo wandered closer to where Lors sat, still mumbling to himself. Lors had several bits of spare clothing crumpled around his bedding, along with some crumpled bits of paper and several trinkets.

"May I see your papers?" Ivo asked, not

willing to just grab them. He doubted Lors would react well to that.

Lors brightened, his face lighting up. "Yes, yes!" He grabbed the crumpled pages, spreading them out and smoothing the wrinkles from each page. They turned out to be playbills, small posters advertising upcoming plays and performances at a downtown tavern. "They're pretty!"

The art wasn't bad, Ivo conceded, but he didn't know about pretty. "Very." He gave Lors a smile, noting that there were several scribbles and notes on the corners of the pages. One of them even depicted the sigil that had been carved into the side of the containers that held bodies. So the witch was having Lors do everything except cast the spells on the crates. Were the rest of them meant to hide bodies or transport people who were still alive?

"Thank you for letting me look," Ivo said. He stood again, and Lors continued to smooth wrinkles from the pages, smiling down at them.

Walking back over to the barrels, Ivo inspected the empty ones. They didn't have any marks, however, which made Ivo think that the sigils had been carved after the people from Adamore had arrived. Maybe the witch had needed more energy to cast the spells on the warehouse.

"Anything useful?" Hansel asked.

"No," Ivo said. "Wait. Maybe. He's got a bunch of playbills with notes on them. They're all for one tavern. That could be a lead, if Jasper or this witch are operating out of there or frequent there."

"Better than anything else we've got," Hansel said. He looked about ready to say something else, but the back door opened again, and two army corpsmen entered, followed by Rosalie. They all looked wet and were dusted with a layer of snow and ice, and neither looked at all pleased to be dragged out in the weather.

It took more time than Ivo liked to explain the matter, and it was only after Rosalie vouched for him as a witch hunter that he got anywhere. The corpsman in charge didn't look pleased to have the mess dumped in his lap, but he promised to take care of the warehouse, its contents, and Lors, as well as to let Ivo know if anything turned up that would help him in tracking down the witch.

It was nearing dusk when he, Hansel, and Rosalie left the warehouse, and the sleet had turned to snow. Underfoot, the slush had turned to ice, making the going treacherous as they headed back to Rosalie's shop.

"Would you like to come in, have another cup of tea?" Rosalie asked. She smiled at Ivo, then hastily added, "Both of you, of course. I'm sure you'd like to dry off before you head to your inn."

"Best to keep going and not have to dry off twice," Ivo said, returning her smile. He clasped her hand briefly. "Thank you for your help. Hopefully we won't need to bother you again."

"Please don't hesitate to drop by if you do need me again," Rosalie said. She glanced away, seemingly nervous. "Or if you just want to chat."

"Of course," Ivo said. He gave her another smile and then bid her goodnight, heading down the street with Hansel. They reached the inn they'd booked rooms at after a long, treacherous walk, the snow not stopping as they travelled. Thankfully they made it without incident, though both Ivo and Hansel nearly toppled several times after slipping on ice concealed by the snow.

"What do you think we should do next?" Ivo asked as they entered the inn and headed toward the room they'd rented. It was close to the center of the building, so there was plenty of warmth to it. It had three small beds, and he and Hansel had dumped their packs on the third one. "We could go find this tavern tonight, but I'm not certain this Jasper or anyone else will be out, given the weather."

"Probably not," Hansel agreed. He sat down heavily on the bed in the middle of the room, scrubbing a hand through his snow-wet hair and making a face. "I don't want to be out in this weather, either."

"Tomorrow, then," Ivo said. "Hopefully the staff will know Jasper. If not, we can go back and see if Rosalie has any further thoughts on where we could look next."

"You could have stayed," Hansel said, his expression carefully blank.

"Stayed where?" Ivo asked. He sat down on his bed to pull off his boots, planning to change into something dry before bed. He'd update his journal and maybe pen a note to Alderling to let him know their progress.

"With Rosalie. She wanted you to," Hansel said. His mouth twisted briefly before his expression went carefully blank. "I think she likes you."

Ivo snorted. More like she wanted to talk magic with him. At least she'd seemed to recognize that he hadn't told Hansel about his magic. That was probably the source of Hansel's displeasure, that Rosalie was nice and had magic and wanted to spend more time with them. He likely wanted as little to do with magic as possible, which only reinforced Ivo's decision to keep his magic on the subtle side. He'd cross the bridge of sharing it with Hansel only if he had to.

"She reminds me of my mother," Ivo said. "She just wants to help. Particularly since people are getting killed."

"If you say so," Hansel said, then added, "Your mother, really?"

Ivo laughed, stripping off his jacket and throwing it at the third bed in the room. "Yes, really. You might want to put on dry clothes before you catch a chill."

Hansel grumbled, but thankfully left off the topic of Rosalie. He changed quickly, and if Ivo snuck a glance here and there, well, Hansel didn't notice and that was all Ivo was going to get. He wasn't stupid enough to try to build anything more, especially given Hansel's opinion on magic.

# Chapter Twelve

The tavern was called The Dancing Swan, and it was set in the center of the market area. It was one large, sprawling building, with a stage set up in the back of the tavern room and a wide swath of floor given over to tables and chairs. It was bustling, even given the terrible weather that had followed Ivo and Hansel across town. Ivo and Hansel set themselves up at a small table near the stage, which was empty and would be until later that evening, according to the flyer that was sitting on the center of their table.

A server appeared after a moment, plunking down two cups of beer without asking. "You just drinking, or do you want food too?"

"We'll take food," Ivo replied. "Thanks."

The server nodded and walked away, collecting a few empty cups and plates from other tables before heading to get them the requested food. Hansel scoured the tavern, but if he saw anything out of the ordinary, he didn't say. Ivo glanced around, but he doubted anyone involved in this affair would be stupid enough to stand out in a crowd like this.

He reached out his magic, feeling for any spells, but the only thing he encountered was a simple spell to block vermin from entering the tavern. A smart spell to have. The server returned after a moment, dropping two plates of steaming food in front of them before immediately wandering off to drop off more beer at a nearby table.

"What now?" Hansel asked with a scowl. "Are we going to sit here all day and hope someone shows up?"

"No," Ivo said. He picked up his fork and dug into the food in front of him. It was hearty and well-flavored, even if he didn't particularly enjoy the food most taverns served. Sipping at his beer, he glanced around the room. "Eat, and then we'll ask some questions."

Hansel shifted impatiently but did as Ivo directed. He looked as though he wanted to spring from his seat and go shake answers out of everyone. As they ate, Ivo studied Hansel's face. He hadn't shaved in a few days and was looking a little scruffy, with a half-grown beard and wild hair. His clothes were wrinkled, as were Ivo's, one of the side effects of traveling for so long without access to laundry.

He was still more compelling than Ivo cared to think about. His eyes were sharp with intelligence and his smiles were genuine, and he cared so fiercely about his sister it made Ivo's chest ache. He wanted to find Hansel's sister, but he was fairly certain this quest was going to end in sorrow—both for Hansel, when they found his sister, and for Ivo, when he eventually had to reveal his magic and lost all of Hansel's trust.

He'd tell Hansel in a heartbeat if he didn't think it would run Hansel off. The last thing he needed was to try and track down this witch with Hansel also doing so. That seemed a recipe for disaster.

They ate quickly, and Ivo was nursing a second cup of beer when the server came back around to collect their plates.

"Excuse me," Ivo said before they could walk off. "I'm sorry to bother you, but my friend and I are looking for someone by the name of Jasper."

"Jasper," the server repeated. Their eyes narrowed briefly before they shrugged. "Sorry, don't know anyone by that name."

"Can you check with the rest of the staff?" Ivo leaned toward her, smiling a sharp smile. "See, my friend here is trying to borrow some money off me to pay money he owes Jasper. Only, he's not so good with making sure money gets where it needs to go, so I'm making sure it does."

The server's expression shifted, and Ivo wasn't sure they were going to take the bait. They nodded and walked off as quickly as they'd arrived, and Ivo turned back to Hansel.

"Did you have to say that?" Hansel asked, scowling a little.

"They know something. There was recognition in their face when I mentioned Jasper, but they're probably not letting just anyone find him," Ivo said. "But someone owing Jasper money? That's a positive reason to let us see him."

"But did you have to make it sound like I'm too stupid to manage my own money?" Hansel asked. He wrinkled his nose but didn't seem too put out.

"It explained your scowl," Ivo said, grinning. "Besides, how else would I explain that I have no idea what Jasper looks like?"

"Well, neither do I," Hansel said. He didn't look too concerned about that. Before he could say anything else, a man appeared at the side of the table. He was far better dressed than most of the people in the room, including Hansel and Ivo. His clothing looked tailored to him, and he wore several rings on each hand, which was asking for trouble, but maybe he thought he had nothing to worry about. His hair was neatly clipped, and he had a goatee that made him look older than he probably was.

"I heard you were looking for Jasper," the man said.

He was Jasper, Ivo was sure of it. He hadn't expected Jasper to show up; he'd expected to be directed to wherever Jasper was, or told to come back later to meet Jasper.

"We are," Hansel said. He smiled sharply, standing up. "I have a business proposal for you."

"Do you," Jasper said. His eyes narrowed, and Ivo followed Hansel's lead, standing as well. "That's not what I was told."

"No, it likely wasn't," Hansel said. "Shall we take this somewhere... quieter?" He glanced around the room, underscoring the fact that the room was full of people, and plenty who were close enough to overhear.

Jasper didn't respond immediately, then jerked his head to the door that led to the back and headed that way. Ivo gestured for Hansel to lead the way, content to let him take the lead for the moment. Jasper strode through the crowded tavern, disappearing out the back door.

Outside was a small yard, empty of other

people and coated in a layer of ice and snow. The snow was still falling, but Jasper didn't seem to notice, despite not wearing a proper jacket. Ivo reached out with his magic, feeling out any spells. Jasper was wearing one, likely a protection charm from the feel of it, but nothing malicious that Ivo could sense.

Not that it would mean much if Jasper had his own magic, as Ivo suspected. If he wanted to cast a malevolent spell, there was nothing stopping him. Ivo really wished he'd had a chance to replace his own protection amulet, but wishing wasn't going to help him here. He'd just have to be vigilant.

"What's this business proposal, then? Be quick about it, I've got too much to do to waste time on idiots," Jasper said. He crossed his arms, obviously considering them idiots.

"We saw your operation by the docks," Ivo said when Hansel hesitated. "We want in."

Jasper snorted. "I don't know what you're talking about. I have a lot of business ventures down by the docks. You're going to have to be more specific."

"People," Hansel said. "You're moving people."

Jasper's eyes narrowed and he said, "You're mistaken. If you'd kindly take yourselves back to whatever hole you crawled out of—"

"No," Ivo said. "I have it on good authority that you've been moving people for magical uses. We want in, or we're going to the law."

"Go to the law, then," Jasper said. He crossed his arms, his mouth twisting. "See if I care. You don't know what you're talking about."

"Then why are you still here?" Ivo asked. "We've talked to Lors. We know all about you."

Jasper grimaced. "Is this blackmail, then? What do you want?"

"We want in," Ivo said again. "There's got to be a lot of money in that sort of business."

"Maybe," Jasper said, his eyes narrowing again. "Unless idiots like you bring the authorities down on us, like you did at the warehouse. You think I don't know about that? And you two think you can just show up here and demand in after costing us one of our hubs? No, you won't be seeing anything from this venture any time soon. You'll have to make up for screwing up that depot."

Ivo glanced at Hansel, whose face had darkened. He looked ready to strangle Jasper, shifting his weight restlessly. "I don't know anything about that. It can't have been our fault."

"Sure," Jasper said. "I'll believe that as soon as I believe that you want to join me in my ventures."

Ivo had barely registered the words when Jasper lifted his hand and lobbed a spell at him. He couldn't believe Jasper was casting attack spells in such a public place—but they weren't *really* in public, there were no witnesses—and Ivo was knocked off his feet as Hansel barreled into him.

Hansel let out a yell as the spell hit him, curling away from Ivo, and Ivo could smell the sizzle of the burn of the spell. He didn't hesitate, drawing up his own magic and throwing a spell back at Jasper. It was a simple but effective spell, one meant to incapacitate the target. It would have hit Jasper square in the forehead, but his amulet flared up, taking the hit. Ivo scrambled to his feet, already pulling together another spell, but Jasper had turned to flee back into the tavern.

Ivo lunged for him instead, tackling him around the knees even though the impact jarred through him like he'd run straight into a wall. Jasper swore as he fell, cracking his head on the side of the building. Ivo scrambled, half climbing, half crawling until he could pin Jasper down and prevent him from getting up.

"Don't move," Ivo snarled. Jasper scowled up at him but didn't follow the order, struggling and trying to get his arms up to fight back. Ivo placed his hand square on Jasper's chest and pulled together a spell, letting it settle softly through Jasper's body. Jasper glared at him but stopped moving—because he no longer could. Ivo had frozen everything below his neck.

"I don't know if you're familiar with this spell," Ivo said, slowly getting up. "It's open-ended, and if I don't remove it, it will spread. First you won't be able to move your head, and then you won't be able to talk. Then you won't be able to breathe. Usually it's a toss-up between whether the suffocation gets you or if your heart will stop first."

Jasper swore at him, hatred burning in his eyes. "I won't tell you anything."

"Suit yourself," Ivo said. He turned away from Jasper toward where Hansel was still, not moving, and Ivo's heart stuttered until he saw that Hansel was still breathing. Two quick steps brought him to Hansel's side, and he knelt down, carefully touching

Hansel's shoulder.

Hansel groaned, making a face. "It's fine. I'm fine."

"You're not," Ivo said, his heart beating rapidly. There was a scorch mark burned darkly on Hansel's side. It had eaten through his jacket and all the layers of clothing beneath, and Ivo's stomach turned at the burn that had blistered the skin from Hansel's hip to his ribs, stretching across his front slightly.

"It looks worse than it is?" Hansel said. He tried to sit up, but only grimaced and dropped back to the ground. "I'll be fine."

"Right," Ivo said. He was torn: should he leave Hansel and Jasper and go for help? But if he did, he'd likely lose the chance to get any information from Jasper. Well, he could at least relieve a little of Hansel's pain, even if he couldn't do much else. "Hold still."

Hansel frowned. He wasn't moving much anyway, his breathing shallow, and Ivo held his hand out over the burn and carefully loosed a small amount of magic into it. Healing magics were difficult and more often caused more damage than they did help, but there were a few small spells that Ivo knew that would help. If he'd had his parents' shop, or even Rosalie's shop, he could make something to take the pain out and speed the healing, but all he had was his magic.

"Ah!" Hansel gasped, his chest expanding suddenly. He stared at Ivo with wide eyes. "What was that?"

"Magic," Ivo said softly. "I can't do much, but

that should numb the pain. Do you want me to go find a healer? Or can you wait until I've talked to Jasper?" Hansel's expression darkened, and Ivo stifled a sigh. He really had been overly optimistic that Hansel wouldn't find out about his magic, and obviously he hadn't been wrong about Hansel not being receptive to it.

"Talk to him," Hansel bit out, carefully sitting up. He winced, his hand hovering over the wound in his side. His face was pale, and he didn't meet Ivo's eyes, staring down at the wound.

Well, the sooner Ivo got what he needed out of Jasper, the sooner they could get that wound taken care of. Hansel would likely disavow him, but that was a problem for later. "Keep still and let me know if I need to go get help." Ivo wasn't sure that was the best option, but Hansel had seemed sure enough.

"Ready to talk?" Ivo asked, his voice hard as he stepped over to Jasper, who glared at him. His mouth twitched, and hie was jerking his head slightly, but obviously the spell was working as intended, as he couldn't move it more than a twitch.

"No, and fuck you," Jasper snapped. "Take this damn spell off of me, or I'll make sure you both burn."

Ivo laughed darkly. "No, that's what you'll do if I take the spell off. I hope you don't think I'm that idiotic."

"Maybe not," Jasper said, the twitch of his head stilling involuntarily. "But you're going to regret every second of the rest of your life once I'm free."

Ivo smiled but didn't say anything. He sat down on the ground next to Jasper, crossing his arms and waiting. Jasper glared at him, staying quiet. Ivo continued to wait. He could always loosen the spell if he needed to, but Jasper could suffer. Ivo tried not to listen to Hansel's ragged breathing behind him, focusing on Jasper and the way more and more of his face slowly stilled.

"What do you want?" Jasper finally rasped, his breath catching in his throat as he spoke.

"To know everything," Ivo said. "But first, where do I find your boss?"

"She'll kill you," Jasper said. "She won't wait. She'll find you and tear you limb from limb. The pain you'll feel will be nothing like you've ever—"

"Where?" Ivo asked, ignoring Jasper's attempts to intimidate him.

Jasper stayed quiet for a long moment, then, his face grimacing, said, "North. Kuflach. The Bischofstein farm."

"Is that where all the people from Adamore were sent?" Ivo asked. "Or are you sending them other places too?"

"Adamore?" Jasper repeated, gasped, and sucked in a haggard breath.

"It's south, near Surstuhl," Ivo said patiently. He didn't loosen his spell, letting Jasper suffer. "There were nearly two dozen people living there."

"Oh, that one," Jasper said. "Yes, most of them go there."

"And the rest?" Ivo asked. That one. How many towns had this group annihilated? Jasper didn't answer, and Ivo jabbed his fingers into Jasper's leg to remind him that he could still feel things. "And the rest?"

"I get some," Jasper snarled. "Some don't make it."

"How many towns have you decimated?" Ivo asked. "Adamore isn't the first time you've done this." Jasper coughed, and Ivo reached out his magic, loosening the spell slightly. Jasper looked like he might not answer, and Ivo prompted, "I can speed the spell if you're done answering questions."

"I've only been working for her for three months. I know she's done it before, but Adamore was the first time I've been involved." Jasper jerked his chin. "You may as well kill me now. As soon as she finds out that I've helped you, she'll come and kill me herself."

"We'll see." Ivo said. He stood, roughly shoving Jasper out of sight of the door. He drew up his magic again, settling a light sleeping spell on Jasper. That done, he stepped back inside.

The server who had fetched Jasper for them was nowhere in sight, which probably didn't mean anything good. Ivo sighed, gesturing for another server to come close. He held up a gold coin. "Can you spare a few minutes to run me an errand?"

"Of course, sir," she said, beaming. "What can I do for you?"

"I need a message sent to the King's Army outpost," Ivo said. He pulled out his notebook, scrawled a quick note, and gave it to her. "Speed and discretion are important. When you get back, come out back and I'll see to it you get this." He tucked the gold coin away and pressed a silver one into her hand as a guarantee that he meant business.

"I'll be back as quick as I can," she promised.

The coin and the note disappeared into her pockets, and Ivo waited until she'd fetched a jacket and disappeared out the front door before returning out back. Jasper was still where Ivo had left him, as expected.

Ivo took off his jacket as he exited the door. The cold bit into his skin, but he ignored it, walking over to where Hansel was leaning against the side of the building, his eyes closed. Ivo knelt down, gently laying his jacket over Hansel's injured side. Hansel grumbled but didn't open his eyes. Hopefully he would be quick to mend.

Hansel wouldn't like it, but Ivo would call on Rosalie. She'd be able to help more than Ivo could. She had the materials, and Ivo didn't think Hansel would be quick to mend otherwise.

Several tense moments later, the server returned, a woman dressed smartly in the uniform of the King's Army on her heels. Behind her were two additional guardsmen, both looking like they'd rather be elsewhere. The server looked extremely curious, but she took the gold coin Ivo held out without hesitation and disappeared back inside without any questions.

Ivo took a few minutes to explain what had happened. The woman didn't seem surprised. Apparently she'd heard about the warehouse incident the previous day and had verified his name on the list of active witch hunters maintained in each major city.

"You going to be making any further trouble around town we should know about in advance?" she asked. Her guardsmen had picked up Jasper and were making off with him.

"Not that I know of," Ivo said. "We'll be heading north before too long, I promise. The spells on him," Ivo jerked his head toward Jasper, "should wear off in a few hours."

"All right. When you're finished with this witch hunt business, I want a full copy of your report to Captain Alderling as well." The woman turned and followed her guardsmen off, not waiting for a response.

Ivo made a note of that, and then turned to Hansel to figure out how he was going to get Hansel to Rosalie for help. He'd downplayed the damage, sure Hansel wouldn't want to wake up in the King's Army outpost, especially since they generally eschewed magical assistance in their healing. Too much history of things going wrong.

# Chapter Thirteen

Ivo yawned, listening to the crackle of the nearby fire. He set the book in his lap down, glancing at Hansel. Nothing had changed: Hansel was still laid out on a pallet in front of the fire, a blanket pulled up to his waist. He wore a loose shirt that was unbuttoned and open down the front to give him some warmth but leave his wounded side open to the air.

The wound was slathered with an oily poultice that smelled of mint and bergamot, a combination that Ivo wasn't particularly thrilled by. It did seem to be working, however. The blisters had mostly receded, leaving a wide swath of angry red that looked painful but seemed less dangerous.

Rosalie had since gone off to bed upstairs, after Ivo had insisted he was fine downstairs. He should be trying to rest himself, especially since he had a good two days of walking to do to get to Kuflach and would be leaving in the morning at first light. Rosalie had heard of it, though she hadn't heard of the Bischofstein farm. He'd leave Hansel here so he could recover, and hopefully he'd be able to travel quickly enough that there would still be some of Adamore's residents left to save.

Ivo refused to think about whether Gretel

would be among them. He hoped so, for Hansel's sake. If the witch at the farm was truly the one in charge, then no doubt she saved the people who would give her the most power for herself. She'd likely given Jasper the men in the warehouse for his own ends.

Hansel groaned, stirring. Ivo stood up and went to fetch the soup he'd left by the fireside to keep warm in case Hansel woke. He knelt next to Hansel just as Hansel's eyes fluttered open. He looked up at Ivo with no recognition for a brief moment, and then his eyes sharpened and he tried to sit up.

"No, don't," Ivo said, putting his free hand on Hansel's shoulder even as Hansel winced and lay back, one hand going to his burned side.

"Ow," Hansel muttered. He took a deep breath, his hand still hovering over the wound. "What happened? Where are we?"

"At Rosalie's," Ivo said. He set the bowl of soup down on the floor next to Hansel. "If I help, do you think you can sit up? You should probably eat."

Hansel grunted an affirmative, and Ivo grasped his hand, helping him slowly sit up. He moved a chair in closer so that Hansel could lean against it, and then sat on the floor next to him.

"Jasper hit you with a nasty spell," Ivo said. He paused, because that wasn't really true. "Thank you. If you hadn't pushed me out of the way, I would have taken that hit."

Hansel lifted a shoulder, taking the bowl of soup when Ivo handed it to him. He was quiet as Ivo described what he'd learned and what Rosalie had done to treat the burn wound. Hansel ate slowly as

Ivo talked, every so often wincing when he shifted or breathed the wrong way.

"What do you mean, you're leaving me here?" Hansel demanded when Ivo finished. He set down his bowl, glaring at Ivo like he wanted to strangle him.

"You're not fit to travel," Ivo said, because it was true. "I'm sure you don't want to travel with me, anyway."

"What?" Hansel's glare only darkened. "What does that mean?"

"Well, you certainly didn't seem happy about... me being a witch," Ivo said, haltingly. He shouldn't be upset. There was no reason to be upset. He'd known that was how this was going to play out for ages. "It's probably for the best we part ways. If I find your sister, I'll send her back—"

"You think I'm upset you're a witch?" Hansel asked, incredulous.

"You're not? Because you certainly didn't seem happy about it yesterday!"

"I was injured!" Hansel said, his voice raising. "Why would you assume my reaction was to anything but this?" He gestured to his side, wincing.

"You... well, you're from a small town, and the only magic you've run into has been black magic," Ivo said, trying to explain while still reeling that Hansel didn't seem to want him to go as far away as possible. "And you weren't exactly nice to Rosalie..." Ivo trailed off, glancing upstairs. "Which, she is upstairs, so maybe keep your yelling down unless you want to wake her."

"Shut up," Hansel said, his voice quieter but

no less angry. "I don't like her much, but that's not because of her magic. I thought..." Hansel trailed off, then grimaced, his hands flexing in his lap as though he wanted to brace his side. "I figured you might have magic. I wasn't sure until you cast at Jasper, but I thought asking was rude."

"It's not," Ivo said, still not quite wrapping his head around the knowledge that Hansel didn't care he was a witch. "Wait, so why don't you like Rosalie?"

Hansel shrugged, looking down. He frowned. "I'm grateful for this, don't get me wrong. And I am going with you. You can't leave me here. I'll follow after you even if it makes my wound worse."

"I could make you stay," Ivo said. He knew plenty of spells that would keep Hansel incapacitated.

"You won't, though," Hansel said. He took a deep breath, wincing. "I need to know if Gretel is alive. I can't just wait here and hope while you risk your life to find out for me."

Ivo hesitated. On the one hand, he felt for Hansel, and if he let Hansel come with him, there was less of a chance that Hansel would injure himself trying to catch up. On the other hand, if Hansel stayed here, he'd be safe and not get in the way of any future spells that might injure or kill him. Ivo liked the idea of him being safe.

"Please?" Hansel asked. "I know I'll be slower than usual, but I need to know. What if she's dead?"

"How about we decide in the morning?" Ivo asked, stalling. Maybe there was something Rosalie could do to further dull the pain or speed the healing. Ivo doubted it, but that was better than telling Hansel no outright. Maybe she could help convince Hansel that it was better for him to stay here.

"Ugh," Hansel muttered. "Fine." He took a deep breath, then made a face. "Help me lay back down?"

"Sure," Ivo said. He didn't rub that in Hansel's face, just helped him. Picking up the empty bowl, he stood. "You need anything else? More food?"

"No," Hansel said. He had arranged himself much the same as he'd been lying earlier, with the wound clearly visible and exposed to the air. It looked terrible, and Ivo was convinced all over again that he should leave Hansel here, where it was safe.

Taking the bowl to Rosalie's little kitchen, Ivo took a moment to breathe. He splashed his face with water, his mind racing. He wanted to say yes to Hansel, even though no was the better option. He could always take the coward's way out and sneak out while Hansel was asleep. He'd make it to Kuflach far before Hansel did... but what if Hansel seriously injured himself coming after Ivo? That would eat at him the entire trip.

Drying his face, Ivo sighed and tried to still his swirling thoughts. Maybe Rosalie would have a solution for them in the morning. Ivo returned to the main room, not surprised to find Hansel was asleep again, snoring softly. Ivo smiled faintly and went back to the chair where he'd been keeping vigil. Settling in, Ivo draped a blanket over his lap and tried to find a comfortable way to fall asleep.

*~*~*

Morning dawned too quickly. Ivo woke to soft voices talking, the smell of tea, and a nasty crick in his neck. Groaning softly, he rubbed at his neck and frowned at Rosalie and Hansel, who were sitting not far away. Rosalie was kneeling in front of the table that Hansel sat on, carefully applying a poultice to his side. Hansel winced, but the redness of the wound was far less ominous than it had been the previous day.

"Is that any better?" Rosalie asked. Neither appeared to have noticed Ivo was awake, so he stayed still, watching Hansel breathe.

"I don't feel it as much," Hansel said. "I can feel it, and it hurts when I move, but it's... like there's something blocking most of it. I'm aware of it, but not really feeling it, if that makes sense?"

"That's good," Rosalie said. "But you have to be careful, because while you can't feel it as strongly, it is just as injured. You'll have to pay close attention so you don't strain it or make it worse."

"I'll be careful," Hansel promised. He glanced at Ivo, his mouth twisting into a lopsided smile. "Morning. Rosalie was patching me up so I can travel with you."

"Ugh," Ivo muttered. "I need tea or coffee before I can discuss this."

Rosalie laughed, standing up gracefully. "Stay there, Hansel, and let that ointment work in some more."

"Sure," Hansel said. He ran his fingers around the edges of the wound, holding himself stiffly. "I should be fine to travel. It's just walking."

"Just walking," Ivo repeated, not convinced.

"There's a lot of movement involved in walking, plus your energy is going to be taken up by healing. You'll need more breaks..."

Hansel shrugged. "I'll make it work. I'm coming with you."

"Ugh," Ivo repeated, giving Rosalie a smile when she brought him a cup of coffee. She had tea for Hansel, and disappeared again before returning with another cup of tea for herself. "Thank you, Rosalie. I'll make sure you get plenty of recompense—"

"I'm sure you will," Rosalie said cheerfully, sitting down in a chair near Hansel. "How's it feeling now?"

"The same," Hansel said. "You think it'll be fine, right, Rosalie?"

"No," Rosalie said. "I think you're going to go whatever I say. That's different."

Ivo snorted, smothering his smile in his cup of coffee when Hansel shot her an aggrieved look.

"Take a spin around the room," Rosalie suggested, not bothering to hide her smile. "See how it feels then."

"Right," Hansel said. He set his cup of tea down and slowly stood. He'd lost his shirt entirely, and Ivo tried not to stare too much at his bare chest, the well-defined muscles in his shoulders and back, the firm ass below that back...

"Well?" Rosalie asked.

"It's not bad," Hansel said. He'd walked slowly, stiffly, and obviously it was going to be a slow trip with him along. Ivo didn't think he had a choice: either he went with Hansel and was able to help him, or Hansel would follow after him and injure himself further trying to keep up.

"I don't believe you," Ivo said. "We're not leaving today."

Hansel opened his mouth, then shut it, his brow furrowing. "But you are letting me go with you."

"Do I have a choice?" Ivo grumbled, making Rosalie laugh again.

"I don't think you do," she said. "That's all right, though. I can make you some protection amulets if you're leaving tomorrow, and I can show you how to apply some of the healing poultices, Ivo."

"You don't mind us staying here?" Ivo asked. "I'm sure you've got other clients to tend to as well."

"You'll pay me well," Rosalie said, grinning at him. "King's Army and all that. I'm sure they give you plenty of budget to work with."

Ivo rolled his eyes, finishing off his coffee. "Yes, you'll get paid." Ivo stood, running a hand through his hair and fighting a yawn. He still wanted to sleep for another day, but there were some things he needed to take care of. "I'll go get our things from our inn, and stock up on a few things. Hansel, you stay here and rest. Walk some, though. You don't want to stiffen up by not moving."

"I could come with you," Hansel suggested. "That'd be a good test."

"Start smaller. We can go for a longer walk later," Ivo said. He headed toward the door, grabbing his jacket. "I'll be back in a bit."

Rosalie and Hansel chorused their goodbyes, and Ivo left the little house, the cold breeze and falling snow waking him far better than the coffee had. Shaking off his stray thoughts, Ivo walked through town to the inn where they'd been staying.

It was two full days before he and Hansel hit the road. They probably could have left sooner, but Ivo was being overly cautious. If Hansel made his wound worse, then that would slow them down more than staying an extra day in Wolueik would. The weather had partly influenced that decision as well; it had been snowing hard the day before, so it had been an easy decision to stay at Rosalie's for another day.

"Remember the deal," Ivo said as they left the city.

"Like you'd let me forget," Hansel said. He was walking more slowly than he had been on the trip to Wolueik, but he seemed all right despite the still-livid mark on his torso. Rosalie had given Ivo several poultices and spells to help ease the pain and speed the healing, so hopefully that would keep Hansel going.

"Next time let me take the hit, and then you can pester me," Ivo said. He grimaced as the wind picked up, wishing again it were summer so they wouldn't be dealing with cold and snow. Travel was a lot easier when he didn't have to worry about frostbite, but black magic witches weren't particularly known for being reasonable.

They traveled in silence after that, the wind and the snow making conversation next to impossible. Ivo made sure they stopped regularly, despite Hansel's grumbles. Around midday, he had them stop for a longer break, building a fire in the shelter of a stand of trees not far from the road. It cut the wind, though not entirely.

Ivo had Hansel sit near the fire and undo his jacket and shirt. He inspected the wound quickly, not surprised to find it was looking worse for the travel. He didn't say that, however; that was a discussion they'd had before, and there was no point in rehashing it. Applying more of the poultice Rosalie had given him, Ivo murmured the spell words, keeping his touch light as he fed energy into the poultice.

"How does that feel?" Ivo asked, drawing away.

"Good," Hansel said, his voice rough. He dropped his gaze to his shirt when Ivo met his eyes. He cleared his throat. "Can I cover up?"

"Yeah," Ivo said. He cleaned his hand off with a handkerchief, then busied himself with building up the fire some. They'd rest here for a while, even if it wasn't the warmest of spots. He wanted the poultice to get a chance to work itself in and take some of the inflammation out of the wound.

Hansel didn't disagree when Ivo told him such, and they passed an hour or so drinking tea and huddling next to the small fire before getting on the road again.

It took them two and a half days to get to Kuflach, and they likely only managed that because the cold weather made stopping a miserable experience. Hansel was looking a little worse for wear, but he insisted a good night's sleep somewhere warm would help immensely. They'd spent the two nights on the road bundled together, the closeness a slow torture of what Ivo would love to have, but even that hadn't kept them warm.

Kuflach seemed a little smaller than Wolueik, though it looked as though it had been thoroughly planned out from its inception. The roads were laid out in a grid, with blocks of near-identical buildings inhabiting each stretch between the streets. It was easy to find the center of town, where several inns and taverns were clustered together. Everything was buried in snow, but someone had seemingly gone through the whole town to carve neat little paths between all the buildings.

Something about it raised the hair on the back of Ivo's neck, but he couldn't put his finger on what. He picked a building with bright lights and a sign out front advertising rooms for let and approached it, Hansel on his heels. Inside, the building was as brightly lit as it had been outside, the tables arranged neatly. There weren't many people inside, likely due to the weather.

The proprietor approached them, a wide, short man with an easy smile and more teeth than he had hair. He set them up with a room upstairs near the fireplace, not questioning when Ivo requested only a single room. He wanted to keep an eye on Hansel, to make sure he was healing properly.

Upstairs, the little room was basically what Ivo had thought it would be. There was a large bed, no windows, and the warmth of the chimney from the massive fireplace downstairs made the room plenty cozy. The room also had a writing desk, which was unusual, but Ivo had seen odder. They'd barely set their bags down when someone knocked.

Ivo opened the door and accepted the plates

of food with a smile to the young woman on the other side. She stammered out for them to let them know if they needed anything else, and then fled back downstairs. Ivo shook his head but brought the meals inside and set them on the writing table.

Hansel had already stripped off his jacket and shirts, leaving his torso bare. Perhaps that was what had had the woman fleeing; Hansel was no chore to look at, even with the barely-diminished wound on his side. Ivo had had plenty of time to look at it—and feel it, which wasn't helping his peace of mind at all.

"It doesn't look much better," Ivo said. He crossed the room, fetching the poultice from his bag.

"It feels better. If it's like any of the other burns I've gotten, it'll stay red for a long while," Hansel said. He skated his fingers across it, leaning down to look at it. Ivo supposed he was the better judge; it was his wound, after all.

"So long as it is feeling better," Ivo said. He knelt next to the bed, leaning in so he could apply the poultice. Concentrating, he murmured the spell that Rosalie had taught him, warmth wending through his fingers and spreading across Hansel's skin. He could see Hansel relax under his touch, and he carefully spread the poultice, keeping the spell going as he did so.

He'd only been doing it twice a day, but he felt the strain. Ivo rarely used his magic. He didn't have nearly the strength his sister did, and he'd never bothered to learn more than basic spells. Using it even just a few days in a row was taxing. Hopefully that wouldn't cause any trouble when they confronted the witch.

"Tomorrow we'll look for the witch," Ivo said. He tried not to think about it too much. He'd already obsessed about the many ways this could go wrong, particularly going against a witch who had so many victims at her disposal. At least Rosalie had been able to give them protection amulets to break the first nasty spell the witch cast against them.

Hopefully that would be enough. If it wasn't... well, he'd sent an update to Alderling before they'd left Wolueik. It would be up to the King's Army to finish this witch.

"Do you think she knows we're coming?" Hansel asked. He shrugged his shirt back on, doing up the buttons in the front.

"Probably," Ivo said. He didn't doubt word of Jasper's capture had made its way to Kuflach. How, he wasn't sure, but Jasper had known about Lors, so likely they had some way to keep tabs on each other. "Not much we can do about that. We'll just have to be extra careful."

Hansel nodded, not looking particularly happy with that answer, but Ivo wasn't happy with it either. Standing, he fetched the plates of dinner he'd set on the writing table and passed one to Hansel. They could get a good night's rest and figure the rest out in the morning.

# Chapter Fourteen

The morning dawned bright, the sun shining and no trace of clouds in the sky. It was almost a welcome change from the snow they'd faced the entire trip, except that it brought the bitter cold back with it. Ivo led the way out of the inn, stuffing his hands in his pockets.

They'd dodged the proprietor's questions on why they were in town. Ivo wasn't sure who to trust here, not when there was a witch setting up operation. Someone in town had to know, and someone in power was either looking the other way or actively helping.

Hansel was moving without any hesitation, any lingering soreness from his wound gone. That, or he was really good at pretending. Ivo was inclined to think the former. Even a great actor would slip up sometimes, and Hansel had never particularly struck him as a thorough liar.

"Where do you think this farm is?" Hansel asked. "There's a lot of ground to cover."

Ivo frowned thoughtfully as they walked. "Not south. We came from that direction, and it was mostly wooded. Maybe if we find the marketplace, they'll be able to point us in the right direction without tipping anyone off."

"Maybe," Hansel said. He didn't sound very convinced, but Ivo didn't take that personally.

They spent the next few hours poking around town, pretending to be looking for local specialties for a shop in Roesschot. Hansel played his part beautifully, falling into line with Ivo's half-truths and lies easily. They got several answers and learned of several farms in the area, but no one mentioned the Bischofstein farm.

Ivo accepted a cup of warm cider from Verena, the woman who owned the small shop they were in, taking a sip and giving her a smile. "This is amazing."

"Thank you," she said, beaming. "It's a family recipe, passed down from my great-great-grandmother. Shame we don't make enough of it to sell to a big city like Roesschot, but I prefer to keep the business in the family, anyway."

"So no other places you'd recommend we ask after?" Ivo asked, leaning on her counter. "I heard something about..." He frowned, pretending to cast for the name.

"Bischofstein Farm," Hansel supplied. He gave Verena a smile. "Someone mentioned it, but we didn't get a chance to ask after what they're famous for."

Verena's expression clouded, no longer open and happy. "I'd stay away from there, if I were you. I've heard nothing but rumors, mind, but I've never heard a good thing about that place. The whole family is odd, and now they've got even stranger people coming and going at all hours, bringing deities know what through our city."

"Maybe that's why they were discussing it,"

Ivo said, grimacing. "Where are they at, so we don't end up there?"

"Northeast of the city. They have a ridiculous manor house and several barns they don't use any longer. Used to be big into sheep, from what my ma told me, but they haven't done that in decades." Verena made a face. "No, you'd want to visit the Frathenal farms. They'll have more of what you're looking for. They dabble in the cider, like me, but mostly they put out the most amazing wool. You'll want to stop by there for certain."

"A few others have mentioned them," Hansel said. "They'll be our first stop, though I doubt their cider is anywhere near as good as yours."

Verena smiled at that, any lingering discontent at the mention of the Bischofstein farm disappearing from her countenance as they continued to chat.

Half an hour later, Ivo and Hansel were stepping back into the cold, their breath misting in the air as they walked away from Verena's cozy little shop.

"Northeast, then?" Hansel asked, pitching his voice low. They weren't likely to be overheard where they were, but better safe than sorry.

"Let's go," Ivo said, his stomach knotting. He wasn't relishing this confrontation. Somehow he doubted it would go as well as their last few had. Though if he was being honest, the confrontation with Jasper hadn't exactly gone well. "Unless you want to rest? We have been going hard the last few days."

"No," Hansel said, as Ivo had expected. "I

want to get this over with."

Ivo nodded in agreement, shoving his hands into his pockets and walking with Hansel along the road that led north. The town was laid out in such a way that the streets at the center of town only went north-south or east-west. They walked along the north road for a while before cutting east, the roads slowly widening and becoming more hazardous with more ice and snow clinging to them. They made it out of town in an hour, though it probably would've taken less time if the roads had been clear.

Outside town, they followed the road, passing one small farm that looked to mostly be in the sheep business. Not the one Verena had pointed them to; this one was too small to be anything but local. Past that, Ivo and Hansel followed a well-maintained fence, spotting the manor house Verena had mentioned past a large, empty field. There were several barns not far from the house, all large and equally well cared for.

Ivo felt out with his magic, but if there were any spells on the buildings, they were too small for him to note from so far away. The grounds were empty, and Ivo kept walking, Hansel sticking close as they continued down the road.

They reached the entrance to the farm after a few more moments of walking. Ivo kept going, frowning at the open gate. The manor house was set far enough back from the road that anyone who glanced out the windows would see them coming. There was no cover between the gate and the house or the fence and the barns.

"I don't like this," Ivo said softly, though he

wasn't sure who he thought would overhear him.

"I like the idea of coming back at night even less," Hansel said. "Maybe we could pretend we're lost travelers?"

"Only if you want the witch to think we're easy prey," Ivo said. "She kidnapped an entire town for her own uses. Why wouldn't she take advantage of a couple of travelers?"

"It could be a way to get close without raising her guard," Hansel suggested. "Or we could try and sneak around from behind the barns. Maybe there will be people inside we can get to help us."

"Maybe," Ivo said. He kept walking, glancing over his shoulder at the buildings in the distance. He liked the second option better; he didn't like the idea of confronting the witch head-on. "Let's walk the road a little further and see if there's any cover behind those barns, or anything else that might interfere with sneaking up behind the house."

Hansel nodded his agreement and they continued to walk. There was no movement from the houses or barns. There was nothing he could pinpoint as unusual about the house or barns, but the whole place made the hair on the back of his neck rise. The road curved off to the left, the fence staying straight, so Ivo stopped there. He surveyed the fields.

Everything was covered in unbroken snow. No one had walked the fields in at least a few days, though given the lack of divots in the snow, it had likely been even longer. If they went this way, their tracks would be obvious to anyone who looked.

Ivo looked up, squinting at the bright sun. It was just past noon, so the sun was starting its trek westward. If they crossed the snow plain from that direction, anyone looking wouldn't see their tracks for the sun glare. They'd just have to get across the field before they were seen.

"I think if we head around and come from behind the barns, we have the best chance of approaching unseen," Ivo said. "If we can get across the field without being seen, the sun will keep anyone from seeing our tracks."

"We can play the lost travelers card if we do get caught?" Hansel suggested. He was already making his way toward the fence, and Ivo followed after him, readying his knives for a quick draw.

They hopped the fence and made their way across the field as quickly as they could. It was difficult going, the unbroken snow hiding a solid layer of ice that required slower movements than Ivo liked. He kept a close eye on the buildings as they walked, but there wasn't so much as a flicker of curtain as they grew closer.

Perhaps the witch wasn't home. She could be off gathering material for spells, be it people or other ingredients. Ivo didn't want to trust that, however, and he came to a stop as they finally reached the first of the barns. There was a large, open door on either end, and Ivo took a deep breath, edging toward the door.

"Ready?" He asked when he reached it, glancing at Hansel.

Hansel nodded grimly, his mouth set in a firm line.

Ivo peeked around the corner, but there was no one in sight. Edging into the barn, he looked around more fully. The barn had obviously once been used to house livestock. Horses, probably. It was empty now, with no sign of the animals that had previously inhabited the space. Instead, there were several wagons and several coffin-like boxes that were empty, their lids set beside them.

They walked the length of the barn, and Ivo reached out with his magic to search for any hidden spells. There was nothing to be found, but he could sense several spells nearby that were strong and unpleasant.

"Do you see anything?" Ivo asked, but Hansel shook his head. They peered at the manor house, but there was no sign of anything wrong there. The curtains were drawn, which was odd this time of day, but it could be simply that the residents weren't at home.

"Let's check out the next one," Hansel said. He started to walk toward the entrance facing the manor house, but Ivo grabbed his arm.

"Out the back," he said, tilting his head toward the way they'd come in.

"Right." Shaking his head, Hansel headed back that way, the stone floor crunching underfoot. They made their way to the next barn quickly, and Ivo didn't like the look of this one. He felt it out with his magic, wincing at the acrid feel of several malevolent spells inside. They seemed to be grouped toward the center of the barn, so it was unlikely that they'd trigger a spell by entering the barn.

"Careful," Ivo cautioned Hansel anyway. The door on this barn was shut, and Ivo eased it open with Hansel's help. They both winced at the sound it made, a creaking, grinding scrape as it edged open under their hands.

Ivo slipped inside before Hansel could, intent on taking the brunt of any spells, but nothing happened. Inside, the barn was dark, the door at the front closed as well. Ivo could hear breathing, but no one protested their entrance. Turning back to Hansel, he said, "Let's open that all the way."

Hansel turned and shoved the door hard, not waiting for Ivo to help. Sunlight spilled across the interior of the barn, highlighting the bodies and people filling the room.

Ivo winced. The bodies were laid out right next to one another, husks of humans who had been drained of life. They still wore whatever clothes they'd been kidnapped in, and obviously the witch cared not for whatever they had on them, as Ivo spotted several pieces of jewelry and other bits that she could have sold for money.

Hansel stepped past Ivo into the barn, staring down at the bodies with a blank face. Ivo had no idea what to say, so instead, he focused on the people he could still help. Further into the barn there were still several people alive. They were tied up, though to what end given they were sleeping the sleep of the bespelled, Ivo didn't know. There were a dozen of them: four men, six women, and two children who looked to be seven or eight. Their wrists and ankles were bound together, and they all had a scrap of fabric wrapped around their necks that had the sigil to make them sleep.

Ivo frowned, studying the sigil more closely. There was nothing in the spell to sustain the people it was causing to sleep. Maybe that was why they were bound? The witch could come in, drop the spell, make them eat and drink, and then put them back to sleep until she needed them.

"She's not here," Hansel said, making Ivo jump. "Sorry. I don't see her. None of these... none of the bodies are hers."

"Do you recognize anyone else?" Ivo asked. Were the people from Adamore here at all? Or had they been taken elsewhere? Though there was one more barn for them to search.

"Maybe," Hansel said. He sighed, running a hand over his face. "I didn't run into too many people from Adamore, not often enough to be certain that any of these people are from there. Gretel is the only one I'd recognize in a heartbeat."

"Let's go check out the other barn," Ivo said. "Maybe she'll be in there."

Hansel nodded. He didn't move immediately, jerking his chin toward the bound people. "Are you going to free them?"

"Not yet," Ivo said. "I don't want to alert the witch that we're here, and breaking her spell will certainly do that. I'd hoped we'd find them unspelled."

"That would be too easy," Hansel muttered. He walked back toward the door they'd left wide open. The warmth of the barn was seeping away quickly, something that must have been a spell on the barn, but Ivo didn't shut the door behind them. Either they'd be back to free the people inside, or the witch would kill them and check on her 'supplies' before they could get too chilled.

The third and final barn was not far off. Ivo led the way, feeling out for spells. There were none on this barn or inside, and Ivo considered telling Hansel that and steering him away. That wouldn't do Hansel any favors, however. At this point, even if it was Gretel's body they found, Hansel deserved to know.

The door on this barn was open as well, and Ivo's breath caught in horror as they stepped inside. Inside this barn were more bodies. Lots more bodies. There were three or four dozen, laid out as neatly as they had been in the other barn. There were no living people, and Ivo's heart ached for the number of people who had been killed here. How had Alderling known about the atrocities near Surstuhl but not known about this?

A question Ivo was definitely going to demand answers to the next time he saw Alderling.

Hansel was walking among the bodies, his mouth set in a grim line as he stared down at each withered corpse. Ivo followed, his anger growing as he noted the children tucked among the bodies. It was hard to distinguish between the adults, how old they had been and how much life they'd lost, but the children were easy to see.

The door at the other end of the barn was wide open as well, and Ivo walked toward it, careful to avoid the bodies covering the floor. The manor house was stately, if old fashioned in its build. It was two stories tall and had been painted white, with a darker stain on the windowsills and the porch that faced the road. The curtains were faded in the windows, showing some sort of pattern, but the colors were lost in the bright sunlight.

As he watched, one of the curtains in the lower level twitched. If he hadn't been staring at the house, he would have missed it. Frowning, Ivo fixed his gaze on that window. The curtain moved again, a hand and arm appearing briefly, as though someone was leaning on the windowsill from inside the room.

The arm disappeared again almost immediately. Someone was home.

Ivo turned, nearly jumping out of his skin when he found Hansel had snuck up on him and was right behind him.

"She's not here, either." Hansel scrubbed a gloved hand through his hair, making it stick up at odd angles. "Where could she be?"

"I don't know," Ivo said. He glanced at the house. "That's the only place we haven't searched."

"You think she might be inside? But why? Everyone else, dead and alive, is out here," Hansel said. He glanced back over the barn, his mouth twisting unpleasantly. "Unless you think she brings them inside to kill them."

"Maybe," Ivo said. "I really don't know, though. Until we get in there, we won't know."

"So what now? Pretend to be lost travelers?" Hansel didn't look too thrilled about that option, and Ivo agreed it probably wasn't the best route.

"No," Ivo said. "Let me think a minute. I don't think approaching the house is a good idea. I can tell there's spells on it, even from here, and that's where she'll be strongest."

Hansel crossed his arms, scowling at the house. "So we lure her out?"

"Probably the better idea," Ivo agreed. "Come on, let's go back to the other barn."

They made the trip back to the other barn in silence, Ivo's head swirling with ideas on how to approach this. They couldn't simply leave and come back later. For one, the witch could very easily leave and set up shop elsewhere by the time they reached a town with any sort of reinforcements that could assist. There was no way she wouldn't know that someone had snooped around. Their tracks in the snow aside, they'd left all sorts of prints around the barns.

If they left, she'd also likely kill off the remaining people who were still alive, and Ivo couldn't stomach the idea of any further people dying at this witch's hands.

If he broke the spells on the people in the barn, that would alert the witch, and she'd come investigate. Maybe if he broke just one, she'd think it was a fluke and come out with her guard down.

That was the best plan he could think of. Storming the house was out. Approaching the house would only make her defensive. No, their best bet was to get her outside somehow and surprise her.

"I'm going to wake one of them," Ivo said as they entered the second barn. "Hopefully the witch will think one of her spells failed, and then she'll come out to reset it without thinking something is up."

"You think that will work?" Hansel asked. "Maybe we should wake them all and create enough of a distraction that she'll be so busy focusing on that she won't notice us."

"If we do that, she'll know there was magical interference," Ivo said. Though it wasn't a terrible idea. If he could figure out how to rig it so that all the sleeping spells came undone after she was out of the house, that could be useful. If only Hansel also had magic, they could do it together. "Maybe once she's close enough to attack more directly."

Hansel nodded, frowning down at the people in front of him. "Who first, then?"

Staring down at the dozen people still asleep in front of him, Ivo frowned. One of the adults, that was for certain, but which one? They all looked pale and sickly, as though they hadn't had proper nutrition in a long while. None of them would be helpful in a fight against a witch—or any fight, really.

"Go stand by the door. Out of sight from the house," Ivo directed. He knelt down next to the woman who had the best color, carefully resting his fingertips against the sash around her throat that held the sigil. Reaching out to the spell, he started to slowly unravel it, hoping to emulate the way a spell would deteriorate if it was sloppily applied.

The woman woke, tensing immediately, and Ivo shushed her before she could say anything. "Quiet now. We're here to help, but I need you to help us. Stay here, try to wake your companions, and we'll deal with the witch. Understand?"

She nodded, her eyes wide, and she sat up as Ivo stepped away. He moved to the other side of the barn door, and they waited. The woman he'd woken shook the man who was laid out next to her, tears welling in her eyes when he wouldn't wake. Ivo left her to it, feeling bad that she wouldn't be able to wake them.

From the house came the sound of a door slamming shut, and Ivo tensed, drawing his knives. Across the barn, Hansel had pulled out his own wicked-looking hunting knife.

# Chapter Fifteen

Ivo could hear the witch's footsteps long before he could see her. He could also hear her muttering curses as she made her way toward the barn. Superficially, it seemed as though the ruse was working.

The witch stepped into the barn and then immediately stopped.

She was breathtaking. Her hair was long and vibrant, bouncing into curls where it stopped around her waist. Her skin was smooth and unblemished, young and unwrinkled. She didn't look a day over twenty, if that. There were several jewels on her fingers and more around her throat, and she wore a dress that was more befitting a royal ballroom than a small farmhouse on the outskirts of a small city.

How old was she really? Ivo didn't linger on the question, lunging for her. On the other side of the barn door, Hansel did the same.

The witch took a step back, her mouth dropping open into an O, but she wasn't surprised for long, and before Ivo or Hansel could reach her, she flung out her arms and cast a spell that had them tumbling backward. Ivo fell to the barn floor, cracking his head against the rocks. He didn't wait to gather his wits, scrambling to his feet and readying a spell.

"What do you idiotic fools think you're doing?" The witch snapped her fingers, and the knives Ivo still held came flying out of his hands. They and Hansel's knife clattered to the floor at her feet. "Is it just you two? I would have thought you had more, given how much your fool stunts have disrupted my network."

"We won't be the only ones," Ivo said. "Even if you kill us, more will come."

"Let them," the witch said. She waved her hand, dragging Ivo to the side of the barn where Hansel was. She clenched her fist, and Ivo suddenly found himself unable to move. Ivo pushed against the spell, but it didn't budge. Hansel glowered, and Ivo really should have gone for help. They weren't going to help the people here, not if they were dead.

Walking closer, the witch peered at them both, her eyes stunning in their vibrancy. Stolen from the deaths of at least a hundred people. Probably more. Ivo's anger only grew, and he wished he had come up with a better plan than 'ambush her when she came in the door.' Obviously she was far better practiced at magic than he'd realized, and he should have realized, given the number of bodies he'd seen.

"You're a handsome one," the witch said, tapping her finger against Hansel's cheek. She frowned, and even that expression was pretty. "Why do you look familiar, boy?"

Hansel spat at her, the glob of spit landing on her cheek. The witch reeled back, obviously not having anticipated that response, and the spell around Ivo loosened. He pushed with his magic, putting all he could into it, and the spell snapped. It rebounded, both at Ivo and at the witch.

The witch stumbled back another step, her eyes widening. She managed to say, "oh," and then Hansel's fist slammed into her cheek. Ivo followed that up with a stunning spell, his head spinning at the use of so much magic with so little energy left. He fumbled through his pockets for the third knife he kept there. It had to be in there.

Despite the spell, the witch stayed on her feet, and she screeched, shoving Hansel back and throwing a sharp spell at him. Ivo could hear it sizzle, and he gave up the search for his knife to pull Hansel out of the way.

They both tumbled to the floor, Hansel landing hard on top of Ivo, and Ivo grunted as the wind was knocked out of him.

"How *dare* you," the witch shrieked, and she raised her hands, preparing to cast another spell, one that undoubtedly would hurt far worse than the one she'd just tried to lob at Hansel.

Then she stopped.

Gasped, her hands dropping to her sides.

Her eyes went wide, and her face seemed to melt, the youth and beauty running away as though someone had poured acid on her face. She tried to speak, but all that came out was a gurgle as she collapsed to her knees.

Ivo stared, then realized there was someone standing behind the witch. A woman, and at first he thought it was the woman he'd freed, but then his head stopped spinning long enough for the woman's face to focus.

She looked like Hansel, and if that weren't enough to cement who she was, the way Hansel cried out and scrambled up—elbowing Ivo in the stomach as he did so—was enough to tell Ivo that this was Gretel.

Hansel threw his arms around her, pulling her in tight, and Ivo took a deep breath, wincing as he slowly sat up. His head spun, throbbing with every beat of his heart, but he ignored that for the moment. Instead, he focused on the witch.

Or rather, the witch's body. While they'd distracted her, it appeared Gretel had come up behind her and buried Hansel's knife in her back. Straight through the heart. She was definitely dead, though that was apparent in the way her skin had withered, all the health and vitality she'd stolen leaving her a ragged husk.

The woman they'd woken was saying something, and Ivo could vaguely hear more voices from her direction. Further proof the witch was dead, since that was the only way the spells that had been keeping the others asleep would have broken.

Ivo scrubbed a hand across his face, opened his mouth to warn Hansel he was about to pass out... but the words didn't leave his mouth, and the next thing he knew, everything went dark.

*~*~*

When he woke, it was still dark, but it was the dark of night. There was a fire burning nearby, and he was warm, despite the bite of the winter cold he could still feel when he breathed. He was bundled up against it. His head was throbbing still, but that was what he got for over-extending himself. It would fade soon, particularly if he managed to get something to eat—and maybe some tea or coffee to drink.

They'd managed to kill the witch, Ivo remembered that much. Gretel was alive, as were a dozen other people. They hadn't failed miserably but had managed somehow, through the grace of the Three. Shifting, Ivo slowly sat up. He was buried in a bunch of fabric, some of it obviously intended to be blankets and other bits not. He thought he recognized some of the pattern of the curtains from inside the manor house.

He was outside, near a large bonfire, and it appeared the dozen people who'd been inside the barn, spelled into sleeping, were also there. He didn't see Hansel, but Gretel sat nearby, bundled in Hansel's jacket and holding a steaming mug. Likely they had made camp outside because going inside the house or staying inside the barn were bad ideas.

"You're awake." She stood when she saw him sit up, passing him the mug she held. "It's a bracing tea. Meant for those who have been sick."

"Thank you," Ivo said, taking the mug. He sipped at it carefully before saying, "You're Hansel's sister."

"Gretel, at your service," she said, smiling briefly. "He's gone to get a wagon or something from one of the nearby farms, so we can get to the nearest town and get everyone some help."

Ivo nodded, several questions fighting for dominance in his head. He took a sip of the tea, recognizing several of the herbs. It was a good mix, particularly for those who were low on energy, magical or otherwise. "Were you in the house?"

"Yes," Gretel said. She sat down next to him. "I was. Nadja—the witch," Gretel clarified at Ivo's blank look, "was using me as a servant. I was hoping she'd give me a chance to kill her before, but she was too careful. I guess when you and Hansel attacked her in the barn, she lost track of the spells she was using to keep me contained. I took advantage of that."

"I'm glad you did," Ivo said. He glanced around, spotting the manor and the barns in the distance. They'd have to go through the house at some point and catalog everything Nadja had been doing. Ivo wasn't looking forward to that. "Hansel was worried about you."

"I was worried about him. I'm glad he had you to help him. I'm sure he would've gotten in over his head at some point otherwise," Gretel said. She smiled as she said it, glancing out at the road. "He should be back soon. Are you all right? Hansel said he didn't see you get hit with any spells, but he thought you might have knocked your head at some point."

"I probably did," Ivo said. He debated mentioning that he'd spent too much energy on spells but decided it would probably be prudent to keep that to himself. Even if Gretel wouldn't mind his magic, he doubted the survivors of Nadja would be happy about another witch in their midst. "Do you know if she was working alone? We found several of her compatriots on the way here, but I'm worried there might be more witches at her level."

"No," Gretel said, shaking her head. "I can tell

you that for sure. She was in charge, and she didn't tolerate anyone else trying anything she didn't approve first. She killed several people who were working for her because they deviated slightly from her orders. I think she was about to kill the witch she had working out near Surstuhl, for some reason or another."

"We took care of her," Ivo said. He'd have to go through all of Nadja's notes and figure out who else might have been involved. That was a problem for a future day. He needed to rest a few days before he tackled that project. Maybe he could get Alderling to send more help for that. Ivo felt he was due a few weeks off for taking out this witch.

"Good," Gretel said.

They lapsed into silence, Ivo drinking his tea and contemplating all the things he'd have to do to clean this up. The more he thought about it, the more he realized he would definitely need more help. Several of the bodies in the barns would be from Adamore, but there were dozens more that he'd need to figure out where they belonged and notify their kin.

He'd never dealt with a massacre of this scale, and he wasn't sure it was something he was equipped for.

"She killed her own family, you know," Gretel said suddenly. "I think they were first. She keeps their bodies in the dining room, arrayed around a table, and she had dinner with them every night."

"That's..." Ivo shuddered. "I can't say I understand that. I've been hunting witches for years, and this is the worst case I've ever worked on."

"How many have you killed?" Gretel asked casually, her hands curled into fists in her lap. Her fingers were bare, and Ivo pulled off his gloves and threw them in her lap. "I don't need to be coddled."

"I have the tea to keep my hands warm," Ivo said. He drank more of it to underscore his point. "To answer your question, dozens. Probably as many people as this witch killed. When my sister and I first started doing it, there were a lot more around. Now I only do it a few times a year."

"That's something, at least," Gretel muttered. She pulled on his gloves, flexing her hands experimentally. "Your sister doesn't do it anymore?"

"No," Ivo said. He smiled, thinking of the nieces and nephews he'd get to see soon. Well, relatively soon. "She's married and settled down. Her husband is a soft city type."

A smile flickered across Gretel's face, and she fell silent again. Ivo wondered what she was thinking, but she didn't say and he didn't intrude. They sat like that for several minutes, until Ivo finished his tea.

"Do you know any of the people who are still alive?" Ivo asked quietly, making sure his voice didn't pitch across the fire. "There were two dozen people kidnapped from Adamore."

"I don't know any of them personally," Gretel said. She sighed, her mouth twisting in an unhappy expression that was so similar to Hansel's that Ivo was momentarily taken aback. "Maybe some of them are from Adamore. She had several... shipments... come in while I worked in her house."

Ivo nodded. He'd ask them later where they

were from. After they were able to get a good meal into them and maybe a good night's sleep. Drawing some of the blankets closer around his shoulders, Ivo fought a yawn. Hansel would be back soon. They could get the people to Kuflach and settled in for the night, Ivo could send a missive to Alderling requesting more help, and then he could get some more rest.

"More tea?" Gretel asked, already standing.

"Please," Ivo said, passing her the mug. She disappeared to the other side of the fire, returning after a moment with another steaming mug full of the herb-filled tea. "You make this?"

"It was one of my mother's recipes. She died when I was young, but she left a book of her recipes and homemade brews," Gretel said, sitting back down by Ivo. "Hansel's worthless for making anything, and this was one of the brews she used to help bolster us when we were sick. I hated it then. Don't like it much now, but at least I can appreciate what it does." She took a sip of the tea before passing it to Ivo.

Ivo took it, amused by the way Gretel hadn't even bothered to ask before drinking from the same cup as him. But then, she had been drinking the tea before she'd given it to him before. He managed to finish the mug and half of another, and was feeling almost human when he heard the sounds of a wagon approaching, the clop of horses and the rattle of the wagon itself.

He stayed sitting, though Gretel stood and approached the gate near the road. A few moments later, the wagon came into sight. It was pulled by two large plow horses, and Hansel sat in the driver's seat, a bulky, unfamiliar jacket encasing him. He got the wagon turned around so that it was facing the way he'd come, and then he hopped down.

"Come on, ladies and gents," Gretel called. "Let's get out of here and someplace warm and safe."

A few ragged cheers came from the group, and Ivo stood, collecting the pile of fabric he'd been draped in. That would serve well to help keep them warm during the trip back to Kuflach. Before he could get two steps toward the wagon, however, Hansel was there.

"You're all right!" Hansel threw his arms around Ivo, the blankets he held and all, and hugged him tight. All too soon, Hansel stepped away. "I was worried. You are all right, right?"

"I'm fine." Ivo smiled, though he knew it was a tired smile. "Just overdid it. I'll be good with some proper rest. You're all right?"

"Better than you," Hansel retorted, his smile infectious. "Come on, let's get back to town."

"Let's," Ivo said. He let Hansel help him into the wagon, ending up at the back. He distributed the blankets and other bits of fabric around the wagon, though the rest of the people in the cart had plenty of their own. Gretel climbed up in the driver's seat with Hansel, and Ivo smiled faintly as they headed back toward Kuflach.

# Chapter Sixteen

"Should you be up yet?" Hansel asked as he sat down next to Ivo at one of the tables in the lower level of the inn they had taken up residence in for the time being. He studied Ivo's face, like that would give him some answer that Ivo wouldn't.

"I'm fine," Ivo said. Fine enough, anyway. He grimaced, taking a swallow of the mellow ale the proprietor served. "I'm just enjoying a different room. The walls were closing in on me upstairs."

Hansel muttered something but didn't argue the point. It had been three whole days since the death of the witch, and the aftereffects of throwing himself out there magically were still dragging him down. Ivo couldn't remember a time when he'd felt so wrung out. Even after his run-in with a witch in Sommervet followed by catching some variant of the summer sweats hadn't left him feeling this wretched.

"Everyone else doing well?" Ivo asked, hoping the change in subject would distract Hansel. "How's Gretel?"

"Acting like nothing happened," Hansel said, rolling his eyes toward the ceiling. "She won't tell me what the witch did to her or if she saw any of the magic..." He hesitated, glancing at Ivo. "I didn't tell her you have magic."

"I don't mind if you do," Ivo said, lifting one shoulder half-heartedly. "She probably saw some of it. She strikes me as an observant sort."

"Sometimes," Hansel said, quirking a smile. "I'll tell her if it comes up, then. Everyone else… well, they seem to be doing as well as they can. A few of them are planning to return home, but most don't have a plan, since most of them came from a small town like Adamore."

No one from Adamore seemed to have survived, from the little Ivo had been able to gather in between excessively long bouts of sleeping. Gretel hadn't had much information on that, but Ivo also hadn't had a chance to talk to her at length. He needed to get back out to the farmhouse and dig through whatever was left to see if he could track down the identities of the poor folk who had been the witch's victims.

"What about you?" Ivo asked. He'd been planning to wait to ask, to get more of a feel for what Hansel—and Gretel, since she was part and parcel of Hansel's plans, no doubt—before he asked. Apparently his mouth wasn't on board with that plan.

"What about me?" Hansel asked, shifting in his seat. He glanced across the room, avoiding Ivo's gaze, and that was answer enough.

"Will you go home?" Ivo asked, even though the thought hurt more than it should. Hansel owed him nothing. It didn't matter that he'd been excellent company, that he'd fit seamlessly on the trip here, and that they worked together well.

That Ivo would miss his smiles. His closeness.

"I don't know," Hansel said. He still didn't look at Ivo. "I don't... I need to talk to Gretel."

So likely Hansel would do whatever his sister did. Something in Ivo's chest twisted. He rubbed at it half-heartedly, then swallowed another mouthful of ale, as though that would wash it away. Ivo didn't push, not wanting to hear that Hansel would be leaving soon. Maybe it was time for Ivo to retire, go back to Roesschot and settle down, spoil his sister's family.

"I don't want to go back to Surstuhl," Hansel said suddenly, glaring at the tabletop. "There's nothing there. But I don't... I don't want to abandon Gretel if she does want to go back."

"You're both welcome to come with me back to Roesschot," Ivo said, his heart hammering in his chest. It didn't mean anything, of course it didn't mean a thing. Hansel would still need to talk to Gretel, and she could say no. "There's plenty of work there. I'm sure Evi would be happy to help you get settled."

"Evi?" Hansel asked, brow furrowing. "Oh, your sister?"

"Yes," Ivo said, smiling. "I'm due to visit them anyway, and I think it's time I took a break from this witch hunting business for a while. A few months, at least."

Hansel nodded, lapsing into pensive silence again. Ivo left him to his thoughts, sipping at his ale and occasionally picking at the bread and cheese in front of him. He needed the energy from the food, but he didn't have much of an appetite. Even just coming downstairs for the meal had left him exhausted.

Hopefully the rest of the aftereffects of over-extending himself would wear off soon. He had too much to do to laze about in the inn for weeks.

He needed to get back out to the farmhouse and see what could be found on the victims. He'd sent another missive to Alderling, but given the weather and the distance, he doubted he'd get a response anytime soon. At least the innkeeper was amenable to housing the people the witch had been holding in thrall. That was another headache, but Alderling would undoubtedly handle recompense for that once he received Ivo's message.

"You look ready to fall asleep in that ale," Hansel commented, giving Ivo a soft smile that made his heart skip a beat. He was obviously getting delirious.

"I feel it," Ivo muttered. He took a hearty swallow, finishing the last of the mug. "I suppose I should drag my sorry self back upstairs."

"I'll walk you up," Hansel said, springing to his feet with entirely too much energy for Ivo's taste.

"Thanks," Ivo said, heaving himself to his feet. "Want to make sure I don't fall down the stairs or something?"

"Or something," Hansel said, snorting. He stayed at Ivo's side as they crossed the room, a steadying presence without hovering too close. As they climbed the stairs, Hansel asked, "What happens next? With the witch?"

"I'll probably go back out there when I'm up to it," Ivo said. He grimaced as they reached the top of the stairs, his head spinning a little at the effort it had taken. "In a few days, maybe. See if there are any other loose ends to tie up. I'm sure Alderling will send out someone from the King's Army to take charge of it, since it's such a... large issue."

They reached Ivo's room—the room he'd been sharing with Hansel. Hansel had decided to stay with Gretel, which Ivo didn't blame him for. To be fair, he'd been asleep more than not, so he hadn't noticed the lack of Hansel for the most part. If it was a bit lonely when he woke, well, that was his problem, and not a new one.

Ivo opened the door, stepping inside and turning back to bid Hansel a good night. Hansel was looking pensive again, his brow furrowed. He opened his mouth, but almost immediately shut it and shook his head slightly.

Ivo frowned. "What's the matter?"

"What?" Hansel shook his head again, this time more strongly. "Nothing. Just... thinking. I'll see you later."

"All right," Ivo said, because there was nothing else to be said—Hansel had turned on his heel and bolted down the hall like he'd been scalded. Sighing, Ivo shut the door and turned back to his bed. He collapsed into it, barely managing to pull the covers up over his head before sleep crashed down on him.

Three days later, Hansel was still being cagey, and Ivo was losing patience. To be fair, he was losing patience with a lot more than Hansel. He was finally starting to feel better, but not well enough that he was up to a trip out to the farm. Several of the witch's survivors were pestering him for more information on what the crown was doing about the witch. The innkeeper was making hints that they wanted to be paid sooner rather than later.

Hansel was avoiding him, which was probably the source of most of his ire. Maybe if he had more energy he'd be able to deal with it all, but he'd only managed to go a full day without sleeping the previous day. That had been a fight, and he was tempted to dive back into bed to hide from it all. That wouldn't fix anything, however, and Ivo was tired of sleeping anyway.

A steaming cup of fragrant tea was set down in front of him, and Ivo glanced up, somewhat surprised to find Gretel taking a seat next to him. She looked better than she had when he'd first met her: there was more color in her cheeks, her hair was neatly braided and shone in the light of the tavern room, and her clothes were clean and fit better than the worn outfit she'd been wearing when they'd killed the witch.

"That'll do you better than this," Gretel said, taking his cup of ale for herself. Ivo snorted but let her. She set down a packet of tea satchels next to the cup, then slouched in her seat like it was a cozy armchair. Ivo wrapped a hand around the cup, raising his eyebrows in question at her. "Got it from the city healer. He said it was good for magic ails."

"Right," Ivo said. He took a sip, not opposed to trying it. There was a floral undertone to the tea, almost buried under far too many spices. It didn't taste bad, at least.

"I want to go with you back to the witch's house," Gretel said. "Hansel said you'd be going back. I want to go with you."

"Why?" Ivo asked. He hadn't expected that, though Gretel seemed made of sturdier stuff than the other victims of the witch.

"I could be helpful," Gretel said, which wasn't a direct answer. "I can show you where she kept her supplies, the spell books she used, where she hid things..."

"I don't doubt you could be useful," Ivo said. "But why do you want to go back there?"

Gretel scowled, taking a long drink of Ivo's ale. Finally, she said, "To prove she doesn't hold any power over me anymore."

"All right," Ivo said. He'd have agreed anyway; there was no reason not to take Gretel along. "I'm hoping to head out there tomorrow. You can meet me down here mid-morning." He'd have preferred to start sooner, but he was sure he wouldn't be getting out of bed first thing. "Let your brother know if he wants to join us, he can."

Gretel's brow furrowed. "What do you mean, let him know? Why wouldn't you?" She sounded suspicious of that for some reason.

Ivo stared back at her, confused. "I've been sleeping enough we're not crossing paths. He's staying with you, so you'll see him before I will."

"He's staying with me," Gretel repeated flatly. Her scowl deepened, and she stood. "Oh, I'll tell him. Excuse me."

With that confusing exchange, she stood and strode off, heading for the stairs that led to the second floor. Ivo stared after her, baffled. Was Hansel *not* staying with Gretel? Shaking his head, Ivo let it go. Hopefully whatever was going on between the siblings would resolve itself before they headed out the next morning.

*~*~*

Ivo took a sip of the bracing tea the innkeeper had given him instead of ale—apparently they'd had a chat with Gretel, and she'd supplied them with several sachets of the tea. Ivo didn't mind. The tea was good, and he welcomed the sharp, bright taste of it. He hadn't seen Hansel or Gretel yet, but if they didn't show, he could always head out to the farm the next day. More rest wasn't going to hurt him, even if he wanted to be moving and doing *something* instead of sitting around.

The lower level of the tavern was quiet: there were a few of the witch's victims settled into one of the corners, playing a quiet game of cards. A few others, who looked to be regular locals. They kept to themselves, occasionally glancing curiously at Ivo and the other newcomers. Ivo finished his tea and stood, leaving the cup on the table with the empty plate from his breakfast. He pulled his heavy jacket on and headed for the front door, intending to track down Hansel and Gretel and get a move on the day.

He still couldn't shake the weird encounter with Gretel. He kept analyzing it, trying to figure out what was going on, but the most he could figure was that they were having some weird spat. Hopefully that wouldn't get in their way on the farm.

The door opened as he was a few steps from it, Hansel all but bursting through, Gretel on his heels. There was snow falling behind them, a scant few flurries, and both of their faces were flushed from the cold.

"Ah, there you are!" Gretel said cheerfully, a smile stretching her face. She gave Hansel a shove. "I told you he'd be up. I need to get something. I'll be right back." She shoved Hansel's shoulder again, then headed for the stairs, taking them two at a time.

"Morning," Ivo greeted. He jutted his chin toward the door. "How's it out there?"

"Just a bit of snow. Should blow over in a few hours," Hansel replied. He shifted nervously, glancing around the room briefly before meeting Ivo's eyes. "Can we talk outside?"

Ivo nodded, stifling alarm. What did Hansel have to be nervous about? Had he and Gretel gone out to the farmhouse without him? Hopefully not, but unless they'd destroyed something, even that wouldn't be terrible. Outside, Hansel glanced around again before leading the way around the right side of the building where the slight breeze was better blocked. The snow was swirling lazily in the wind, but it didn't appear as though much had fallen. That boded well for their trip.

"What's going on?" Ivo asked, leaning against the building when Hansel stopped. He tugged his snow cap down, covering the tops of his ears better.

Instead of answering, Hansel peered at him. "How are you feeling? Are you sure—"

"I'm sure," Ivo said, huffing. "I'm tired, but I'll do better moving around at this point. What did you need to talk to me about?"

Hansel shifted nervously again. He glanced around, then up at the second floor of the tavern.

Whatever he saw seemed to strengthen his resolve. He took a deep breath, looking straight at Ivo. "I'm not sure how to say this."

"I can't help you there," Ivo said with a small laugh when Hansel didn't continue. "I don't know what you're talking about."

Hansel grimaced, shifting from foot to foot again. "I know. I just..." He made a face. "Do you remember, back in Genkerk, when we met with Rosalie?"

"Yes," Ivo said. Was this something to do with Ivo's magic? That had to be it, though what, Ivo didn't know. Maybe Gretel wasn't comfortable with it? Did she know? Ivo's memory of the fight with the witch was fuzzy.

"She was flirting with you," Hansel continued. "She—"

"She was not," Ivo said, flabbergasted. Rosalie had been nice, but she'd only been helping them because that was what good people did. That they shared magic was another bonus. "She was—"

"She *was*," Hansel insisted. "She wanted you to stay with her. I offered to go off on my own, remember?"

"Yes," Ivo said slowly. "You did. She was just being nice, though. What does that have to do with anything?"

Hansel made a face. "I was jealous."

"Jealous?" Ivo repeated. He frowned, trying to figure out what Hansel was trying to say. He was jealous of Ivo? He'd wanted to be flirted with? Or vice versa?

"Yes," Hansel said. He threw his hands up in

exasperation. "You seemed receptive, and she was pretty and she used magic and knew what she was about. I was jealous."

"Oh," Ivo said, feeling like he'd been hit with a load of bricks. "You..."

Hansel groaned, burying his face in his gloved hands. He muttered something that Ivo couldn't make out. Ivo blinked, trying to process. Hansel had feelings for him. That was... not what Ivo had expected, and he rapidly became aware that he was being too quiet. Shoving away from the wall, he almost slipped in the snow, but managed to keep his footing long enough to reach Hansel where he stood a few steps away.

Hansel looked up at him, worry obvious on his face. Ivo didn't bother with words—he'd undoubtedly muck that up—and instead grabbed the front of Hansel's coat and reeled him in for a kiss.

It wasn't much of a kiss. They were both clumsy: Ivo was off balance and Hansel was obviously not expecting it. Ivo stepped back, giving Hansel a grin. "Me too."

Hansel stared at him, dumbstruck. "Really?"

"Not the jealous," Ivo said, "but the rest of it. I didn't think you felt the same. I thought... Well, we were focused on finding your sister. It wasn't exactly an appropriate thing to bring up."

"Right," Hansel said, a slow, happy smile stealing across his face. Ivo mirrored it, a pleasant warmth spreading in his stomach. He leaned in, more deliberate this time. Hansel stayed still, the soft pine-and-cinnamon scent that clung to him still there. Ivo kissed him softly, savoring the closeness and the way he no longer needed to guard the way he felt.

"Come with me to Roesschot?" Ivo asked quietly. He didn't move to put more space between them, but Hansel didn't either. Hansel nodded, and this time he kissed Ivo, as fierce as he'd been when he'd been battling with the first witch they'd faced all the way back in Surstuhl.

Ivo wasn't sure how long they stayed there before the sound of someone clearing their throat broke them apart. Hansel wiped the back of his mouth with his glove, and Ivo grinned at him briefly before turning to see who had interrupted them.

He'd expected Gretel; he hadn't expected Alderling too. He was dressed for the weather and looked to have been out in it for a while, by the accumulation of snow on his hat and the shoulders of his coat.

"Hard at work, I see," Alderling said, his voice muffled by the scarf wrapped around the lower half of his face. Gretel snorted, her wide grin not wavering. "I'll meet you inside, and we can catch up on business when you're ready." Gretel outright laughed at that.

"See you inside," Ivo said dismissively, turning back to Hansel. Alderling and Gretel's footsteps were barely audible as they walked away, but Ivo had more important things to pay attention to.

"Who's that?" Hansel asked, leaning into Ivo. He made no move to follow, and Ivo was content to stay where he was, the heavy weight of Hansel pressed against him a pleasant sensation.

"Captain Alderling. I didn't expect him to

come himself," Ivo said. He sighed, because that didn't bode well. It *was* a more complex situation than Ivo had faced before, though, so it wasn't that odd. "I suppose we should go after them."

"I suppose," Hansel said, laughing softly. He shifted, hooking his arm with Ivo's. "I guess we won't be making the trip out to the farmhouse today."

"We'll see. Alderling might want to see it." Ivo shrugged. He'd never seen Alderling out in the field before, so it was hard to say. "Or he might want to set up camp here. We'd better go find out which."

Hansel slipped his gloved hand into Ivo's as they walked back toward the tavern. Ivo didn't bother to wipe the smile off his face. There were still dozens of things they needed to sort out, but everything was starting to look up.

Inside, Gretel was camped at a larger table by the fire. Alderling was speaking to the tavern owner, who didn't seem quite as surly as she had earlier. Alderling was arranging recompense, no doubt. Ivo took the lead when Hansel hesitated, tugging him across the room to where Gretel sat. She smirked, making Hansel grumble something, but Ivo graciously ignored both, taking the seat next to her.

"Your compatriot seems to have brought half of Roesschot with him," Gretel said once they were seated. "That's more help than we ever got with our witches."

"Ivo came for this one," Hansel said, immediately leaping to their defense. "And—"

"It's only a dozen people," Alderling said, sitting down in the empty chair across from Ivo. "Unfortunately, that's all we could spare. I would have brought more people if I'd had them, but witch hunting isn't a profession that draws many to it."

"I suppose Ivo was better than nothing," Gretel said, tilting a smile at Ivo. "He kept my brother from getting himself murdered."

"Thanks," Ivo said. Hansel shot Gretel a dark look, but she didn't seem to notice. "You really brought that many? There were that many witch hunters in Roesschot when you left?"

"No," Alderling said, nodding his thanks to the server who set down a round of drinks. Ale for everyone but Ivo, who got another steaming cup of tea set in front of him. "Some of them are King's Guard. For... administrative purposes."

Which likely meant dealing with the dead and any notifications that could be done. Grim, but at least they would have help with it.

"We were planning to go out to the farmhouse today to assess the state of everything. We haven't had the chance to go back out due to the weather," Ivo said. He kept his health out of it, though Alderling could likely read between those lines. He was a witch as well, and Ivo had mentioned he'd over-extended himself. "Did you want to do that or settle in and we go out tomorrow?"

"That won't be necessary," Alderling said. "I'm sending you home." Ivo opened his mouth to protest, but Alderling talked over him. "No protests. I've spoken with Ms. Gretel, and she informed me of the sacrifices you've made. The amount of over-extension you've done will take months to ease off, and my team can handle the cleanup."

"That sounds fine," Hansel said, kicking Ivo's

boot under the table. "Ivo wants to show Gretel and me around Roesschot. We agreed it would be better than trying to go back to Surstuhl."

"Sounds like it works out for everyone, then," Alderling said. "Now, give me the full version of what happened, please. All the details you can remember."

"Right," Ivo said. He took a bracing sip of his tea and started with his arrival in Surstuhl and the fire he'd encountered the first evening there. Alderling paid rapt attention, jotting notes in the notebook he carried. Hansel occasionally chimed in with his side. Once they were done, Gretel told her side, which wasn't much: she'd walked into a spelled trap, and the next thing she knew she was waking up in the witch's farmhouse.

It was late afternoon before Alderling was satisfied. Ivo may have overestimated how much energy he'd have. He was tired just from sitting there and talking. He couldn't imagine how much more tired he'd be if he had tried to go through with the plan to visit the farmhouse. Still, *months* of this? That seemed extreme, and he also wasn't sure how he was supposed to travel.

"We're not leaving tomorrow," Gretel said. "I'm going to go with you tomorrow. I assume you're going to visit the farmhouse first thing?"

"Yes," Alderling said. He surveyed Gretel, and apparently satisfied with what he saw, he nodded. "We'll move out first thing. Your experience would be helpful."

"Sure," Gretel said. "The lovebirds can stay here. Maybe Hansel can make himself useful and get some supplies for the trip to Roesschot."

Ivo snorted, grinning at Hansel, who was glaring at his sister like he could make her disappear in a puff of smoke. "We can do supplies together."

"Get supplies for a horse," Alderling said. "I brought an extra cart and horse for your transport. That will allow you to pick up enough supplies for your journey without stopping, as well."

"Excellent," Gretel said. "I think that's a sound plan. We can leave the day after tomorrow."

"Good. Weather permitting, the trip shouldn't take more than a week. I'll visit when I return to see how you're doing, Ivo, and we'll discuss any future matters then," Alderling said. He stood, and Gretel followed suit.

"I'm going to the bathhouse," Gretel said after Alderling walked away to converse with the innkeeper again. "Don't forget, Hansel, supplies tomorrow."

"Yeah, yeah," Hansel muttered. "Go away."

"Gladly," Gretel said. She walked the long way around the table, stooping to give Hansel a quick hug and a kiss to his cheek. With a wave to Ivo, she left them at the table, leaving them alone.

"I take it you both already decided on going to Roesschot?" Ivo asked, taking Hansel's hand and entwining their fingers. Neither of them wore gloves any longer, the fire providing more than enough heat.

"If this," Hansel lifted their entwined hands slightly, "worked out. Otherwise we were going to go elsewhere. Gretel insisted. Maybe back to Genkerk. That was a bigger city. We both agreed we didn't want to go back to Surstuhl."

"We can make a trip out there to get anything you want after the thaw," Ivo suggested. "I don't want you to leave behind anything important."

"Maybe," Hansel said. He shrugged. "Most of what's there will be taken by the villagers when we don't come back. They probably think I ran off with you or that we killed each other in the woods."

Ivo shook his head, but didn't deny it. He yawned, his jaw cracking loudly with the effort. "Something to decide in the spring, then."

Hansel nodded, standing up. He tugged Ivo to his feet, not letting go of Ivo's hand. "Come on. You should get some more rest."

"Only if you stay with me," Ivo said, letting Hansel lead him across the room. "For a while, at least."

"I'd like nothing more," Hansel said quietly, giving Ivo a soft, sweet smile as they headed up the stairs.

Fin

# About the Author

Sasha L. Miller spends most of her free time writing, reading, or playing with all things website design. She loves telling stories, especially romance, because there's nothing better than giving people their happily ever afters. When not writing, she spends time cooking, harassing her wife, and fussing over her cats.